P9-EMQ-755

DANCING
IN THE DARK

**Center Point
Large Print**

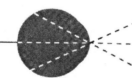

**This Large Print Book carries the
Seal of Approval of N.A.V.H.**

DANCING
IN THE DARK

**Center Point
Large Print**

SOUTH HUNTINGTON
PUBLIC LIBRARY
HUNTINGTON STATION, NY 11746

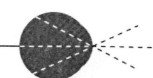

This Large Print Book carries the
Seal of Approval of N.A.V.H.

DANCING
IN THE DARK

MARY JANE CLARK

CENTER POINT PUBLISHING
THORNDIKE, MAINE

SOUTH HUNTINGTON
PUBLIC LIBRARY
HUNTINGTON STATION, NY 11746

LT
M
Clark

This Center Point Large Print edition
is published in the year 2005 by arrangement with
St. Martin's Press.

Copyright © 2005 by Mary Jane Clark.

All rights reserved.

The text of this Large Print edition is unabridged. In other
aspects, this book may vary from the original edition. Printed in
Thailand. Set in 16-point Times New Roman type.

ISBN 1-58547-659-5

Library of Congress Cataloging-in-Publication Data

Clark, Mary Jane Behrends.
    Dancing in the dark / Mary Jane Clark.--Center Point large print ed.
        p. cm.
    ISBN 1-58547-659-5 (lib. bdg. : alk. paper)
    1. Women journalists--Fiction. 2. Young women--Crimes against--Fiction. 3. Ocean
Grove (N.J.)--Fiction. 4. Seaside resorts--Fiction. 5. Serial murders--Fiction. 6. Large type
books. I. Title.

PS3553.L2873D36 2005b
813'.54--dc22

                                                                                2005009355

Once again, for Elizabeth and David.

And for all those who struggle with mental impairment as a treatment or a cure for Fragile X Syndrome draws closer.

DANCING
IN THE DARK

PROLOGUE

Thursday Evening, August 18

Now that she was deprived of sight, her other senses were intensified. She stood in the darkness, seeing nothing but hearing the persistent roar of the Atlantic Ocean in the distance and the soft flapping of wings right above her. Her nostrils flared at the smell of must and decay. The ground was damp and cold beneath her bare feet, her toes curling in the wet, sandy dirt. She felt something brush against her ankle and prayed it was only a mouse and not a rat.

Three days in this dank chamber were enough. If she had to stay any longer, she would surely lose her mind. Still, when they found her, as she fantasized they would, the police would want to know everything. To survive this, she'd have to be able to recount every detail of what had happened.

She would tell the police how he'd leave her alone for what seemed like hours at a time. She would tell them how he'd gagged her when he left so nobody would hear her screams and how he would lower the gag only to press his mouth against hers when he returned.

The police would want to know what he'd said to her, but she would have to tell them that she had stopped asking him questions after the second day of captivity because he never answered. He'd expressed what he wanted by touch. She'd be sure to tell them how he'd caressed her and lifted her up, how he'd maneuvered his body against hers, how she had known she must follow his lead.

As she continued to mentally organize the information the police would surely need from her, she felt a familiar rumble from her stomach. She had eaten sparsely of the meager provisions, but that didn't really bother her. Hunger was a familiar friend. She knew the ability to survive with minimal sustenance was one of her most impressive strengths, though, of course, her parents didn't see it that way. Nor did her former friends or teachers or the health care professionals who had worked so hard to steer her away from the path she had taken. They didn't see what to her was only obvious. Not eating was the ultimate control.

As she listened to a pigeon cooing from the eaves above her, she thought more about her parents. They must be frantic with worry. She imagined her mother crying, and her father pacing and cracking his knuckles, over and over, his annoying habit whenever he was upset. Was everyone in town out looking for her? She prayed they were. She hoped that anyone who had ever wronged her, anyone who had ever snubbed her, anyone who had ever hurt her was worried about her now.

The low rumble of the waves rolled in and out, and

she began to rock to the rhythm, trying to soothe herself. It was all going to work out. It had to. She would tell the police what had happened, how he'd silently pulled her to her feet. Without words, he'd shown her what he wanted her to do by the way he moved his body next to hers. She had danced in the dark for him. Danced again and again, trying desperately to please him. Dancing for her life.

Four Hours Later, Ocean Grove, New Jersey

The security guard raised his arm and pointed the flashlight at his wrist. Still an hour to go before his shift was over. Time for one last patrol.

Strolling along the empty paths, George Croft pulled his handkerchief from his uniform pocket, wiping his forehead and the back of his neck. Except for the excessive heat, it was a night like many others in the quiet oceanside town. An occasional throaty snore emanated from the dwellings he passed. The association rules permitted no loud talking after 10:00, and most lights were off by 11:00 P.M. The combination of sun, heat, and salt air had left the summer occupants ready for a good night's sleep.

Finishing up on Mt. Carmel Way, the guard cut across the grass and stopped to check the doors of Bishop Jane's Tabernacle and the Great Auditorium one last time. The massive Victorian-style wooden structures were locked up tight as drums. The illuminated cross that shone from the top of the auditorium, serving as a landmark for passing ships, beamed into the night, signaling that all was well.

He was satisfied that everything was in order, but he still had another fifteen minutes before he was officially off duty. God forbid something happened before 2:00 A.M. and he wasn't on the grounds. He'd lose his job over that. And, although she didn't live in his patrol area, that young woman was still missing. If some sick nut was intent on abducting another Ocean Grove girl, the guard wasn't going to have it happen on his watch.

Lord, it was hot. Longing for a drink of cool water, George turned his flashlight in the direction of the wooden gazebo that protected the Beersheba Well. He knew the first well driven in Ocean Grove had been named for a well in the Old Testament. Beersheba's waters had been good enough for the Israelites back then, and good enough for his town's founding fathers, but he preferred the bottled stuff. Still, the gazebo was as good a place as any to wait it out until his shift was over.

With no breeze blowing in from the ocean, the night air was especially still. He trained the yellow light on the lawn in front of him and walked slowly, trying to kill time. Noticing one of his shoes was undone, he put the flashlight down in the grass and stooped to tie the lace. It was then that he heard the scratching sound.

The fine hairs tingled on the back of his clammy

neck, and George spun the flashlight in the direction of the noise. He squinted, trying to identify what he was seeing. A dark mound, motionless, at least as far as he could see, lay at the base of the gazebo.

George stepped a little closer. Just when he heard the scratching again, he detected slight movement coming from the form. Slowly, slowly, he approached until, finally, the glare of the flashlight reflected off the pale skin of a female face, blindfolded and gagged.

FRIDAY
AUGUST 19

CHAPTER 1

Diane could feel the heat from the sidewalk seeping through the soles of her shoes as she hurried down Columbus Avenue. Beads of perspiration slipped down her sides, and she wiped the dampness accumulating at her brow line with one swoop, negating the twenty minutes she had spent in front of the bathroom mirror with her hair dryer, round brush, and styling mousse. Her freshly laundered cotton blouse stuck to her back, and the starched collar was beginning to droop. The day hadn't even begun and already she was a wilted mess.

She was anxious, as usual, about being late, and she wished she had not promised herself to walk to work. The twenty-block trek was the only dependable exercise she got these days, and she needed it. She had let her gym membership lapse since she found she wasn't using it on any routine basis. There just wasn't time anymore—not if she was going to spend the time she felt she should with the kids right now.

Sniffing the sickening smell of garbage already baking in the morning sun as it waited to be picked up from the curb, Diane felt relief that her two-week vacation was about to begin. It would be great to get out of the city, away from the oppressive heat, away from the noise and the hustle and the pressure. These last months had been tough on all of them, brutal really. Sometimes, it didn't feel like any of it could have happened. Yet the reality was all too clear when she spotted Michelle biting her nails or watched Anthony's shoulders slump when she caught him staring at his father's framed picture on the piano—or when she reached out in the middle of the night to the empty place in her queen-size bed.

She cut across the courtyard at Lincoln Center, stopping for just a moment at the wide fountain, hoping to catch a bit of fine spray. But there was absolutely no breeze to propel the mist her way.

Adjusting her shoulder bag, Diane continued walking. No matter. Soon she and the kids would be someplace where the air didn't stink and the water flowed cool and clear. Maybe they weren't going the way they had originally planned, maybe it wasn't the way they would have wanted it, but it was the way things were. They were going on this vacation. They deserved it. They needed it after all they had been through.

Life, even without Philip, had to go on.

Pushing through the heavy revolving door into the lobby, Diane welcomed the blast of cool air. She smiled at the uniformed security guards as she fumbled in her bag for the beaded metal necklace that threaded through the opening on her identification pass. Finding it, she swept the card against the electronic device that beeped to signal she was cleared to enter the KEY News Broadcast Center. She knew many of the other correspondents found it annoying to produce their IDs. They thought their well-known faces should be enough for entry, but Diane didn't mind. Security had an increasingly tough job, and it was easy enough for her to pull out her card. She did draw the line, however, at wearing the thing around her neck all day. That wasn't a fashion statement she cared to make.

She purchased a cup of tea and a banana at the coffee trolley, then walked up the long, wide ramp to the elevators, passing the large, lighted pictures of the KEY News anchors and correspondents, grouped according to their broadcasts. Eliza Blake beamed from the *KEY Evening Headlines* poster. Constance Young and Harry Granger grinned beneath the *KEY to America* morning show logo. The *Hourglass* photo, taken over a year before, showed Cassie Sheridan surrounded by the newsmagazine's contributing reporters. Diane didn't stop to study her own face, with its blue-gray eyes and nose she wished was just a little bit straighter, smiling from the wall with her colleagues. She needed no reminder. The worry and aggravation of the past few months were showing. The fine lines at the corners of her eyes had deepened, and new ones had formed around her mouth, vestiges of unconscious frowning. Lately, Diane noticed she was forced to apply concealer several times a day to camouflage the dark circles that had developed beneath her eyes.

Another good reason for a vacation, she thought as she pressed the elevator button. If she could just get away and relax for a bit, her appearance would benefit. All of the female correspondents were acutely aware that the way they looked played into their success. It was just a fact of broadcast news life. The guys paid attention to their appearance too, of course. But they could let their hair go gray, sport some wrinkles, gain a few pounds and get away with it. The women couldn't. They groused about it with their friends, but it wasn't going to change and they knew it. For the on-air journalists, experience counted, but youth and beauty were idolized.

The elevator bell pinged, and the doors slid open. Walking directly across the sixth-floor hallway, Diane slipped into the ladies' room. She pulled paper towels from the wall dispenser and patted at her face, trying not to wipe off her makeup as she dabbed at the mascara that had run at the corners of her eyes. As she worked to re-create some semblance of a hairstyle, she heard the click of a lock opening in one of the stalls behind her.

"Hi, Susannah," Diane said as the young woman

limped toward the sink next to hers and pumped out some liquid soap.

"Hey, Diane. Hot enough for you?" Facing the mirror, Susannah smiled her crooked smile, which reflected its way back to Diane.

Diane was about to start complaining about her flattened hair and her sweaty walk to work, but she stopped herself, knowing how insensitive that would be. Susannah would probably give just about anything to be able to take the walk that Diane took for granted.

"Thank God for air-conditioning," Diane answered, pulling strands of ash-blond hair from her brush before putting it back into her shoulder bag. She rifled through the satchel and pulled out a small can of hair spray. "And tomorrow I leave for a vacation with my kids. It may be hot at the Grand Canyon, but it won't be as muggy as it is here."

"That sounds fabulous," Susannah answered with enthusiasm. "Do you have all the information you need before you go? I could get a little research package together for you."

That was one of the great things about Susannah, thought Diane, shaking the can and taking the lid off. She was always so upbeat and eager to help. God knew, Susannah had plenty to be down about. But she didn't play the victim. Maybe she knew that a poor-me attitude wore thin with folks after a while.

"Oh, you're a doll, Susannah, but I don't need a thing. I'm going to just sit back and let the tour guides do their jobs. I'm looking forward to a vacation where

I don't have to read any maps or make any decisions or be responsible for anything more than which pair of shorts to pull on in the morning. I just want to relax with my kids for two weeks and let someone else worry about what we're going to do every day."

Diane waited until the researcher made her way to the restroom exit before pushing the button to release the hair spray. The smell of the aerosol fumes was just reaching her nostrils when Susannah called back from the doorway.

"I guess I should give you a heads-up, Diane. Joel is looking for you."

"Any idea why?" Diane asked as she recapped the hair spray can. But Susannah was already gone.

CHAPTER 2

The detective stood at the foot of the hospital bed in the small examining room, his face impassive as he took detailed notes on Leslie Patterson's answers.

"How many times do I have to tell you?" the young woman's voice rose in frustration. "I never saw his face. I'm telling you the truth. I never saw him."

She watched the detective for a reaction, but his expression gave nothing away. It was the way he was rephrasing the same questions over and over that tipped her off: he didn't believe her.

"Let's go over it again, Miss Patterson. You were on

the boardwalk taking a stroll at midnight?" The detective stressed the last word of his question, signaling his skepticism. "Do you usually go out alone late at night like that?" he asked.

"I told you. I had a fight with my boyfriend and I wanted to be alone to think about things. I thought a walk would clear my head and maybe tire me out so I could fall asleep."

"Your boyfriend would be Shawn Ostrander, correct?"

"Yes. I told you that too." She picked up a spoon from the breakfast tray and threw it back down again. Some nurse had thought she was doing Leslie a favor by bringing in the tray as she waited to be released. *As if I would eat this,* Leslie thought. She sighed as she pushed back the rolling table that held her untouched food.

"And Shawn said he didn't want to see you anymore, is that right, Leslie?" The detective used a gentle tone as he led her onward.

"Yes. And that he'd met someone else." Leslie studied the red marks the plastic handcuffs had left on her wrists and then pulled the cover up higher.

Beneath the hospital blanket, where the detective couldn't see, she pinched the top of her thigh. Without a safety pin or razor blade, a manually inflicted wound would have to do. A hard, mean twist intended to make her feel better. As the pain pulsed, the expression on her face never flinched.

"That must have hurt," said the detective.

Leslie blinked, for a moment thinking the man somehow knew she was pinching herself before realizing he was referring to the hurt of knowing that Shawn had found someone else.

"Yes. It did. I love Shawn." Leslie grabbed again at her hidden flesh and pressed tight. This time, tears welled in her eyes. Not because of the physical pain but because she couldn't stand the thought of losing Shawn. Didn't he realize that no one was ever going to love him the way she did?

"Did you want Shawn to worry about you, Leslie? Did you hope he would reconsider his decision to break up if he realized how much he missed you? Did you hope that disappearing for a couple of days would make Shawn come around?"

Leslie considered her answer. Yes, she did want Shawn to worry about her, and yes, as she'd lain in that dark, damp place for three days and nights, she'd been sustained by the hope that Shawn was missing her. She'd hoped that the horror she was going through would all be worth it because, when faced with the thought of losing her forever, Shawn would realize he loved her as much as she loved him.

But if she told the detective that, it might help confirm what Leslie knew he already suspected. That she had staged a three-day disappearance to get attention. She didn't want him to think that.

"Look, Detective, someone abducted me, blindfolded, gagged, and tied me up, and left me somewhere for three days. I feel like you're accusing me when you should be out there searching for a real criminal."

"We are, Leslie, believe me, we are. I'm not the only man working on this case. The better part of the Neptune Police Department is involved. We will get to the bottom of this. You can count on that." Something in the detective's tone made the words feel more like a threat than a reassurance.

The hospital room door opened, and the doctor who had examined her in the emergency room walked in and stood beside the bed. He looked at his clipboard before speaking. He looked at the cop too. As part of a crime investigation, the police as well as the patient had a right to know these test results.

"The rape kit came back negative. So we have that to be grateful for, Leslie. Even though you didn't claim to be raped, it was good to have done the test. You can never be too sure in a situation like this one. You could have been drugged or knocked unconscious and not even known it." The doctor smiled reassuringly and put his hand on her shoulder. "So, physically, you check out fine. Those scrapes on your wrists and legs will heal in few days. So will the cuts at the corners of your mouth. You can go home, Leslie. You are going to have to talk to someone, though, get your feelings out. Do you need a reference for a therapist? We have some excellent ones on staff."

"Thanks, but I already have a therapist." Leslie nodded, knowing that it made no sense to protest.

Sure, she'd go back to therapy, and she'd fool Dr. Messinger the same way she was fooling the emergency room doctor right now. He had no idea that she was pinching herself, over and over again, beneath the white hospital sheet.

CHAPTER 3

In August, other television news executive producers might be out playing golf in the Hamptons or relaxing in the south of France, but Joel Malcolm was at his desk, clicking the remote control at the half dozen television monitors mounted on his office wall when Diane knocked on the back of the open door.

"Ah, good. You're here," he said, waving her in. Joel nodded toward one of the TV sets. The identifying tag at the bottom of the screen read OCEAN GROVE, NEW JERSEY. A reporter was doing a stand-up report from a beach, the ocean in the background. His face was flushed, his shirt collar was open, and his hair didn't move. If there was no breeze to ruffle this guy's hair, Diane thought, it must be brutally hot, even at the seashore.

"You know about this girl that's been missing from the Jersey Shore?" Joel pointed at the television.

"I haven't been paying that much attention to the story," Diane said, taking a seat on the leather sofa, "but I bet you're going to tell me all about her."

If Joel detected any sarcasm, he ignored it. "Well, she'd been missing for the last three days, but she turned up last night. Matthew got it, off the record, from the local police that they think this girl is making it all up—that she faked her own abduction. Apparently, she's a real head case."

Diane felt her pulse quicken. *Here it comes,* she thought. With *Hourglass* segment correspondents already working on two stories similar to this one, Joel had been rooting for just one more. In Michigan, a college student had disappeared for six days, afterward telling police she had been abducted at knifepoint. In Oregon, two teenage sisters were reported missing after their mother found blood-covered sheets and a broken window in their bedroom. Frenzied searches had been launched for all of them. But police were convinced that the young women hadn't been kidnapped at all—that they'd staged everything.

It was perverse, but Diane was certain Joel coveted another misguided soul, one with her own twisted tale. Someone new and something timely to kick off the show's season opener in September.

"This is perfect for us, Diane. It's a third girl who's cried wolf. I want you to do the story."

"I'm going on vacation tomorrow, Joel," she said, crossing her legs, trying to stay calm, and hoping he had merely forgotten that she had the next two weeks off. Yet she already knew he hadn't. Joel didn't forget a thing.

"This is important, Diane. Your vacation can wait, can't it?"

"No, it can't wait, Joel. This trip has been planned for months."

"You got travel insurance?"

Diane was tempted to lie but thought better of it. One lie always led to another, and usually the truth came out, sooner or later. Lies were what had gotten Philip in so much trouble.

"As a matter of fact, I do," she said. "But I bought it in case one of the kids got sick or something. I didn't buy it to cancel our trip out west so I could work more."

Joel frowned the frown that had intimidated countless other reporters and producers before Diane. The creator and executive producer of the award-winning newsmagazine program was a television legend. With forty years of broadcast journalism experience under his trim belt, he'd gotten to this point by virtue of his quick mind, keen visual sense, and refusal to give in or give up, ever. From his earliest days in the business, when film, not videotape, was the news production medium; even in the days when news lagged hours and, sometimes, days in getting to the public because airline schedules dictated the arrival of newsreel footage in New York before it could be broadcast around the country; in those simpler days before satellites and cell phones and computers on every desk in the Broadcast Center—even when there had been so much less to control, Joel had been a control freak.

Throughout his career he'd wanted everything his way, and he was accustomed to getting what he wanted.

"Changing the subject for a second, Diane . . ." He picked up a pen and began doodling on the yellow legal pad on his desk. "Your contract is up for renewal in a few months, isn't it?"

"In January," she replied, her lips tightening. *The conniving cheat.* This wasn't playing fair. Joel knew her situation and was using it to his advantage. Everyone at KEY News was aware of what had happened to Philip. It had been in all the New York newspapers, it had been on the Internet, it had even been on their own network television and radio news. That Joel was using Diane's misfortune to get what he wanted shouldn't have surprised her; still, she found herself dumbfounded at his audacity.

Joel knew that she was the head of household now. He knew that her salary kept her family fed, clothed, and housed. With Philip gone, she had no other income to fall back on. Though Joel wasn't coming out and saying it, he was clearly trying to tie the certitude of her contract renewal, and therefore the financial security of her family, to her acceptance of this assignment. She resented him for it, deeply.

"Well, you know how these things go, Diane. The front row will come to me. They'll want my opinion before they get back to that agent of yours, who undoubtedly will be lobbying for a hefty pay increase for his star client."

Joel tossed the pen on top of the legal pad. "Of course, I'll want to tell them how valuable you are to KEY News, how important it is to *Hourglass* ratings to have that great-looking face of yours on the screen, to have you delivering our stories. I'll want them to know one of the reasons we have to keep you is that you are such a team player."

Diane leaned forward on the sofa. "Listen, Joel. Can't you please understand? You know my children and I have been through a lot these past months. We all need to get away."

For a moment, she thought the executive producer was actually considering her plea as he leaned back in his chair and stared at the office ceiling. "I'll tell you what," he said. "If you want to bring your kids along with you, that's all right with me. In fact, I'll even find a way to pay for it from our budget."

"You've got to be kidding, Joel. Michelle and Anthony are counting on this vacation. It's the only thing they've shown any enthusiasm for since everything happened. And going to Ocean Grove won't be a vacation, not for me anyway. I'll be working and worrying about getting back to the kids all the time."

Joel tilted his head downward and stared directly at her. "No. I'm not kidding, Diane. This is my final offer. I can make it only because *Hourglass* did so well last season and the finance department isn't about to give me any flak about booking some extra rooms. As for you, I'm sure the quality of your work won't suffer. You're a pro. You can straddle both worlds. That is, if you want to."

She knew Joel was fully aware of the fact that she didn't want to, and she also knew he didn't care. He just wanted what he wanted . . . a ratings winner. Another edition of *Hourglass* that attracted the audience share that determined the advertising rates the network could charge. That was what it was all about for him. His ego demanded that his broadcast remain the nation's premiere newsmagazine show. To feed that ego, he was not beyond bullying when he felt the occasion called for it.

Diane rose from the sofa, knowing she'd lost. She pushed away the thought of breaking the news to her children. They were just going to have to accept the inevitable. She wished they didn't have to learn the hard facts of life so soon, but it was unavoidable, just as the other rough lessons they'd learned lately were. Canceling their vacation out west was another blow, but in the larger scheme of things, it was nothing.

She had read somewhere that children who had tumultuous childhoods could just as easily grow into healthy adults, stronger for their experiences, as develop into maladjusted misfits. Diane prayed every night that was true. Prayed that Michelle and Anthony would benefit from learning early that life goes on despite disappointments. Prayed they'd be resilient and learn to make the best of things. Prayed they'd get a valuable lesson from the example of a mother who was trying to hold everything together and doing what she had to do to support the family.

She had no other choice. With their father in jail, she was all they had.

CHAPTER 4

Helen Richey stood on the front porch, sweeping away the sand from the wooden planks. She found the swishing sound of the broom comforting. It reminded her of the summers of her childhood, when her parents would bring her and her three sisters to spend their vacation here in Ocean Grove. From the weekend after school got out until Labor Day, Helen and her family had lived in one of the tents on the grounds of the Ocean Grove Camp Meeting Association.

Each structure was made up of a wooden porch, an eleven-by-fourteen-foot tent, and a roofed cottage at the rear. Each tent came with electricity, running water, a tiny but complete kitchen, a toilet, and a shower. It was up to the "tenters" to supply everything else: furniture, carpeting, linens, dinnerware, wall hangings, even air conditioners. Some residents brought radios and television sets. Helen's parents hadn't, though. They'd insisted their girls get away from the boob tube, as her father called it, for the summer.

After children's Bible study class in the morning and an early lunch in their tent, the days continued by walking the two blocks to the Atlantic Ocean with their towels and plastic beach toys in tow. Mom would set up a sand chair, attach a portable umbrella to its aluminum arm, and settle in to read her magazines and paperback novels in between shouting cautionary directions to her daughters as they played in the surf. Some days there were lots of waves; some days it was relatively calm. Always there was the fun of digging in the sand, building castles and moats, and choosing a Creamsicle or Dixie cup from the ice cream man.

That was the kind of summer Helen wanted for Sarah and Hannah. Simple, idyllic weeks spent reveling in the sunshine, fresh air, and the glory of the Atlantic Ocean, along with learning some lessons about God and what it meant to be a caring member of a community. She believed childhood summers as part of the Ocean Grove Camp Meeting were time well spent. They helped lay a firm foundation for the adult years. She wished she could make Jonathan understand that.

Her husband couldn't stand Ocean Grove—or "Ocean Grave," as he called it—because if you were looking for excitement, you had to go elsewhere. But Helen knew the town wasn't what Jonathan really detested. It was tent living. He said the primitive and claustrophobic conditions made his skin crawl. He dreamed of a house or condo in another part of town, a place not associated with the religious "tent community."

All summer long he'd managed to come down from their home in Paramus only on weekends. But today

Jonathan was going to leave work early and brave the Friday traffic of the Garden State Parkway to spend a full week with his wife and two children in their tent on Bath Avenue. As much as Helen was looking forward to all of them being together, she was apprehensive as well.

The tents were so close together that sometimes, if a resident of one of them sneezed, a neighbor answered "God bless you." The tents had ears. If Jonathan lost his temper and voiced his opinions in any but the softest voice, the other tenters would know all about his discontent. More than once Helen and Jonathan had been forced to retreat to their car to air their disagreements.

Finished with her sweeping, Helen walked off the porch to inspect the flowers she had carefully planted when the kids and she had arrived in June. Red geraniums, white impatiens, and purple ageratum formed a patriotic border around the base of the tent platform. They complemented the American flag that hung from the wooden post supporting the striped canvas awning covering the porch. The heat was doing a real job on the impatiens, and the little white flowers were wilting and closed. As Helen was about to go fill her watering can at the kitchen sink, she heard the creaking screen door of the neighboring tent.

"Hello, dear," said the frail old woman who stood just feet away.

"Good morning, Mrs. Wilcox. How are you today?"

"Oh, pretty good." Her high-pitched voice cracked.

"A little stiff, but other than that, I'm fine."

"Did you sleep well?" Helen asked, gathering her honey-colored hair and twisting it up off her neck.

"Not really. It was too hot."

"When are you going to get an air conditioner, Mrs. Wilcox?" Helen didn't wait for a reply. "Jonathan is coming down later. He could pick one up and install it for you this weekend." The moment she made the offer, she worried about how her husband would react.

"I don't know, dear. I've always disapproved of having air-conditioning down here. The ocean breeze has always been good enough for Herbert and me. But this year is different. In the thirty-nine years we've been coming down, this summer is the hottest I can ever remember." She nodded back toward the tent. "In fact, Herbert's inside now, trying to take a little nap. He couldn't sleep either, so he got up early and walked over to Main Avenue to get the paper. Herbert said everyone at Nagle's was talking about the Patterson girl."

At the old woman's words, Helen had a sinking feeling in her chest. Fearing the worst, she managed to ask, "Has she turned up? Is she all right?"

Mrs. Wilcox shook her silver head. "She's turned up all right. But the police think she wasn't kidnapped at all. They think she staged the whole thing to get attention."

"Oh, that's terrible, Mrs. Wilcox. Terrible and so very sad."

Everyone in town had been following the story of

the missing young woman, an Ocean Grove native who lived in the community all year round. Leslie Patterson lived with her parents over on Webb Avenue, and just last night Helen had walked with the children to light a candle in front of their pretty Victorian house. After they added their votive to the scores of others on the sidewalk, Helen had used the opportunity to remind the children about the dangers of talking to strangers.

Despite the suffocating heat, Helen felt a momentary chill on her bare arms. Even though she had had the benefit of being raised in a town Helen considered to be just about heaven on earth, Leslie Patterson was one troubled girl. The idea scared Helen as she thought about her five- and six-year-old daughters, who were probably singing "Jesus Wants Me for a Rainbow" in children's Bible study class about now. No matter how carefully you raised your children, no matter how you tried to take care of them and shield them from danger, sometimes they just didn't grow up right.

CHAPTER 5

Trying to keep her face expressionless, Diane held her head high as she left the executive producer's office, but inside she was seething. She resented feeling she had no choice but to take the assignment in Ocean

Grove, resented the fact that Joel had the power to decide her fate. Another correspondent might have told the executive producer to go to hell, but she wasn't that brave, just as she wasn't that stupid.

She needed to have her contract renewed. In a tough economy and an industry that was becoming ever more technologically advanced, jobs at every level were getting harder to come by. Fewer people were needed to get a broadcast on the air. Gone were the days when an experienced television news correspondent could write his or her own ticket, hopping from one network to another.

It would be nice to have the economic security she'd once had. With a husband bringing home a major salary, Diane's slightly lower income had been icing on the cake. The Mayfield family had enjoyed their lives. The spacious co-op in Manhattan, the smaller but well-located cottage in Amagansett, the private schools for the kids. But that was before Philip was indicted. That was before their world fell apart.

Sometimes it still didn't seem possible how quickly things had changed. It had been just four years since Philip landed his dream job as chief financial officer for BeamStar, knowing of the plans to take the cutting-edge telecommunications company public. Diane still seethed at Philip's stupidity, but she was heartbroken at his dishonesty. He had overstated BeamStar's profitability in the papers filed in connection with the public offering. The fact that her husband had done it at the urging of his bosses only angered her more.

When BeamStar tanked, its investors were crazed. The government investigated, and Philip was taken down along with his greedy bosses. Though he cooperated with the investigation, he was sentenced to a year and a day in prison. But with good behavior, he could be out in October.

In the months since Philip had gone to serve his sentence at the federal correctional institution at Fort Dix, Diane had signed the closing papers on their mortgaged beach cottage and taken the profits to pay off some of the fines that had accompanied her husband's prison sentence. She could manage the co-op payments and school tuitions, but there was precious little left over. It constantly amazed her how quickly living in Manhattan ate up what most people in the rest of the country would consider a major-league salary.

As Diane walked into her own office, it occurred to her that maybe she should look on the bright side. Perhaps it was for the best that she was being forced to cancel the trip out west. It cost more than they could afford now, but Philip had insisted they go without him. He felt strongly that she and the kids should take the family trip they had been talking about for years to celebrate Anthony's tenth birthday. Diane had held out for a while but finally reluctantly agreed when her younger sister, Emily, announced she wanted to stay with them for the summer after she graduated from Providence College. Having her sister along as they took in the sights would somehow make it less sad. Even though Emily was closer in age to Michelle and Anthony than she was to Diane, she was a good companion and another adult to fill the void where Philip should have been.

Diane reached for the phone on her desk. She would get her sister on her side before breaking the news to the kids. She might even ask Emily to tell them. Diane didn't want to relay the news to them over the phone, and it was going to be hours before she got home. Instead of packing hiking boots and backpacks, they needed to pack bathing suits and beach towels, and fast. Joel wanted her in Ocean Grove in the morning.

"Knock. Knock."

Matthew Voigt towered in the doorway.

"I can't believe this," Diane groaned. "Come on in and shut the door, will you?"

Matthew took a few steps into the office, closing the door behind him. "So I gather you talked to Joel?" Intense brown eyes sparkled mischievously beneath his dark eyebrows.

"Yeah. He told me."

"I'm sorry about your vacation, Diane," he said as he took a seat in the chair across from her desk.

"It's not your fault. Our fearless leader is a ruthless tyrant."

"Still, it's a bitter pill, huh?"

"I've swallowed worse."

Matthew's mouth formed a wry smile. "Yeah, I guess you have."

Diane sighed heavily, accepting the inevitable and turning to the task at hand. "At least I have you as my producer. That's one good thing."

"Thank you, ma'am." Matthew bowed his head and raised his hand to his forehead as if tipping a hat.

Diane pulled a Sharpie from the cup on her desk. "What do you know so far?" she asked, poising the pen above a reporter's notebook.

Matthew reached out and passed a piece of paper to her. "This write-through gives most of the details up to this point. I've talked to the Neptune police. Apparently, this girl has a psychiatric history, and she pulled a runaway stunt when she was in high school. Turned out she was hiding in a storeroom off the school gymnasium. With this rash of fake kidnappings across the country, the police think the girl's just copycatting."

Matthew waited while Diane sat back in her chair and read the information. Leslie Patterson was twenty-two years old. Her parents had reported her missing when they found her bed unslept in Tuesday morning. Police and Ocean Grove residents had combed the town for three days. Finally, three nights after her disappearance, a security guard found her, blindfolded, bound, and gagged, on the grounds of the Ocean Grove Camp Meeting Association.

"What's the Ocean Grove Camp Meeting Association?" Diane asked, continuing to train her eyes on the wire copy.

"It's some sort of religious retreat. I did a little web research, and it seems the Methodists founded it after the Civil War as a seaside place for worship. Today you don't have to be Methodist to belong, but you do have to uphold the association rules. And get this. The people live in tents."

Diane looked up. "As in canvas?"

"Yep. There are a hundred and fourteen of them. There's a waiting list of a decade or more to get one, and rental rights can be passed down from generation to generation."

"Does Leslie live in a tent?" Diane asked, biting the end of her pen.

"No. A house. She's a year-round resident. The tent people are only there in the summertime."

Diane finished reading the Associated Press account. An unnamed police source had told the AP reporter the investigation uncovered that Leslie had been treated off and on for anorexia, "cutting," and other impulsive behavior. The source said the police were convinced that she'd faked her own abduction as a cry for help.

"Poor kid, huh?" Matthew remarked as she lay down the paper.

"Poor parents, too." Diane shrugged her shoulders and exaggerated a shiver. "Anorexia *and* cutting. Two of a parent's worst nightmares."

"Yeah," Matthew agreed. "But horrible or not, it's perfect for *Hourglass*."

CHAPTER 6

As soon as Matthew left her office, Diane picked up the telephone and dialed her home number.

Her sister picked up on the fourth ring. "Hello?" Emily sounded out of breath.

"Hey. It's me. What are you doing?"

"My abs."

"Good girl." Diane had the mental image of her sister standing barefoot in her shorts and cropped T-shirt as she talked on the kitchen phone. Her short brown hair would be tousled. The ever-present water bottle would be in her hand.

"What's up?"

"I've got bad news, Em."

"And that would be . . . ?"

"We're not going on our trip. I have to work."

"You have *got* to be kidding. The kids are going to freak."

"I wish I were, Em." Diane recounted her conversation with Joel Malcolm and his suggestion that Michelle and Anthony come with her to Ocean Grove while she worked on her *Hourglass* story. "But it really wasn't a suggestion, Em. It was more like an order."

"God, Diane, the kids are going to be so disappointed."

40

"Tell me something I don't know. I'm dreading telling them."

"Want me to do it?" Emily offered.

"I was hoping you might suggest that."

"All right. I'll tell them when they get up."

Diane glanced at her watch. It was after eleven o'clock. She envied her children's ability to sleep so soundly for so long. It would be such a relief not to wake up in the middle of the night and stare at the darkness in her bedroom, to have hours of deep sleep with no tossing and turning. Perhaps nature had planned it that way, knowing that, since the waking hours of adolescence and the teenage years could be so difficult, it would be necessary for kids to have long rests to regroup. Too bad adults hadn't gotten the same pass.

"Thanks, Em. You don't know how much I appreciate it."

"I've got a vague idea."

Diane could sense a knowing smile on her sister's face. Emily had been born an old soul, their mother used to say. Even as a little child, Emily had seemed older than her years. Diane thought there was something fey about the baby sister seventeen years her junior. From the time she began to talk, Emily could figure out people and situations in an uncanny manner. Maybe it was because, as a child, she spent so much time in an adult world.

The sisters talked for another few minutes about what needed to be done. The call to the travel agent to cancel the flight and tour reservations, decisions about what needed to be packed for the new vacation venue. As she hung up, Diane took solace in the thought that Emily would be with her in Ocean Grove. She would be able to work with at least some level of comfort, knowing that her children were not being neglected. Truth be told, she knew Michelle and Anthony had more fun with their aunt than they did with their mother these days.

CHAPTER 7

In Nagle's Apothecary Café, Shawn Ostrander sat on a swivel chair at the Formica counter and asked the cheerful waitress for two cups of coffee to go. The ceiling fans whirred quietly, creating turn-of-the-century atmosphere while moving the air within the old pharmacy turned ice cream parlor and sandwich shop. Though the air-conditioning was cranked up inside, the excessive heat outside blasted through each time the front door opened.

As he waited for his order, Shawn stared at the black ceramic rosettes on the white tile floor, his mind trying to focus on the task at hand. No matter what Leslie had been through, he had work to do this morning. He had to concentrate on his research. But first, Shawn wanted to see if Carly Neath would meet him tonight at his bartending job in Asbury Park.

As the waitress affixed plastic lids to the paper coffee cups, Shawn made his pitch. "It's Guitarbecue at the Stone Pony tonight, Carly. Guitar and barbecue. Wanna come?"

Carly slid the coffee containers into a paper sack and handed it to him. "That sounds like fun, but I have to babysit tonight."

"For who?" Shawn asked.

"The Richeys. Tent people."

"What time will they be home?"

"Not too late." Carly shrugged. "Elevenish, I guess."

"You could come after that," he offered.

Carly looked down at the counter. "I'm kind of surprised you even want to be seen with someone tonight, Shawn," she said in a low voice.

"You mean . . . because of Leslie?"

Carly's blond ponytail bounced as she nodded.

"Look, Carly," he began slowly. "I feel bad about Leslie. I really do. But I can't help her anymore. I have to get on with my life. And I can't worry about what people might think, either."

Carly felt sorry for Shawn as she watched the dejected expression on his face. He'd told her a little about his former girlfriend, and she didn't sound all that stable. But if Leslie had faked her own kidnapping to get his attention, as the gossips were yakking about this morning, Carly felt some responsibility. She knew Shawn had told Leslie that he wanted to see someone else right before she disappeared.

"Okay," she said. "I guess I could meet you there." She felt better as she saw Shawn's face brighten.

"Great, Carly." He grinned. "I'll see you tonight, then, at the Stone Pony. I'm off now to track down Arthur."

Carly looked at her watch. "Oh, I wish I could come with you, but I still have a couple hours to go here."

"Don't worry. I'll tell Arthur you were asking for him."

Carly smiled. "I really enjoyed meeting Arthur the other day, Shawn. I admire you for wanting to help him."

Shawn brushed off the compliment. "It's no big deal, and sometimes, I think I get more out of it than he does."

He paid for the coffee and exited the restaurant, turning left on Main Avenue. Squinting in the glaring sun, he peered out toward the Atlantic Ocean as he walked the two long blocks to the boardwalk.

As he trudged on through the heat, irrepressible thoughts of Leslie clouded his mind. Shawn felt guilty about having broken up with her when she was so needy. He felt ashamed he hadn't joined the search party that had scoured the town looking for her. He was sorry he really didn't care anymore about what had happened to her and was feeling such relief that he was finally done with her.

If anyone had told him the day he met Leslie, when he went to Surfside Realty to find out about a new apartment, that the rail-thin young woman behind the reception desk was going to be so much trouble, Shawn probably would have ignored the warning anyway. He found himself immediately attracted to Leslie Patterson. She was not particularly pretty, not like Carly; but her dark brown eyes pulled him in like magnets. There was a wistfulness to her, as if she was waiting for someone to come riding in to save the day for her.

As he reached Ocean Avenue, Shawn stopped to let the cars pass before crossing over to the boardwalk, telling himself that Leslie was not his problem anymore. Out of pity and a sense of responsibility, he had stayed with her way too long. He'd thought he could help her, cure her, fix her. He'd thought that he could *will* her to get better, that patience and attention and affection would nurse her to health.

What colossal ego he'd had.

Finally, Shawn had come to understand that neither he nor anyone else could make Leslie Patterson well. Her problems went too deep. Much deeper than the cuts she made with safety pins and broken glass behind her knees and into the flesh of her inner thighs.

CHAPTER 8

His conversation with the police had been deeply troubling. Owen Messinger breathed a heavy sigh as he replaced the phone receiver in its cradle.

All the hours of therapy over the last years hadn't made Leslie Patterson healthy. The police believed she had staged her own abduction, an obvious cry for help. Leslie was still a very sick young woman.

Owen got up from his desk and went over to the bookcase, where he pulled out the bright yellow binder from the shelf. Yellow was Leslie's color. The green, red, blue, orange, and purple binders contained the files of the other young women he was treating for eating disorders, self-inflicted wounding, and other impulsive behaviors. Each book contained pages of the therapist's progress notes on both the illness and therapy for his patients.

Taking a seat on the couch that Leslie had sat upon so many times, Owen opened the yellow binder and began flipping through the pages. The entries went back eight years. Leslie had been a high school sophomore when her mother first noticed the razor marks on her daughter's legs. Not the minor nicks inflicted by an inexperienced adolescent shaving her legs but angry slits executed with the sharp edge of the blade.

In his unique brand of shorthand, Owen had scribbled down his impressions:

— *L.P.'S EATING DISORDER = EXTREME WEIGHT LOSS.*
— *L.P. TALKS OF EATING 3X A DAY. CLOSER ANALYSIS SHOWS AMOUNT OF FOOD ACTUALLY CONSUMED VERY LIMITED.*
— *L.P. HAS ENGAGED IN EXCESSIVE STRENUOUS EXERCISE AS A WEIGHT CONTROL MEASURE.*

— *L.P. HAS PERSISTENT PREOCCUPATION WITH BODY IMAGE. SEES HERSELF AS OVERWEIGHT.*
— *L.P. DENIES SEEING HERSELF AS EMACIATED THOUGH SHE IS SEVERELY UNDER RECOMMENDED WEIGHT LEVELS.*
— *L.P. IS TRYING TO RELIEVE STRESS BY CUTTING. UNEXPRESSED OR UNRESOLVED ANGER.*

Owen realized that the notes he had made back then weren't all that different from what he would write about his patient today. Only now he knew for certain that Leslie had expanded her arsenal of cutting tools from razor blades to safety pins and shards of broken glass. And that she wasn't responding at all to the new therapy.

The intercom buzzed, and his assistant's voice came over the speaker.

"Anna Caprie is here, Dr. Messinger."

"All right, Christine. I'll be just a minute."

He closed the yellow binder and slid it back into its place on the shelf. As he pulled out Anna Caprie's grccn book, he hesitated for a moment, wondering if he should continue with his innovative therapy. But he quickly dismissed the thought as he went back to his desk and pulled a package of razor blades from the drawer.

CHAPTER 9

"I'm not hungry." Leslie shook her head as her mother rested the plate on the coffee table. "Why are you always forcing me to eat when I don't want to?"

"I'm not forcing you, Leslie. I'm offering you some lunch. You have to eat something, honey."

Audrey Patterson tried to keep the frustration out of her voice. For the past three days she had made bargains with God. If her daughter was returned to them, if Leslie came home, healthy and in one piece, then she would be more patient with her daughter. She would not nag; she would try harder to be a better mother and friend to her only child. But the initial relief over having Leslie back safe and sound was ebbing away as Audrey felt the familiar pattern reestablishing itself. Three days spent away, God only knew where, hadn't changed things. Leslie was right back to her old behavior.

"Look, sweetheart." Audrey pulled back the edge of the whole grain bread. "It's turkey. The white meat. Nice and lean."

"Please, Mom. Just leave it there, will you? I'll have some later." Leslie pointed the remote control at the television set. With trepidation, Audrey took a seat on the couch beside her daughter as the WCBS noon news broadcast began. The anchorwoman Cindy Hsu welcomed viewers and launched into the top story. A record heat wave was gripping the Northeast. Hospitals were reporting an increasing number of cases of heat-related maladies. People were fainting in the New York City subway. Macadam was melting on city streets. Officials warned of power outages if consumers kept their air conditioners cranked up, and the fire department cautioned that there would be a catastrophe when a fire emergency arose if hydrants continued to be opened by those seeking relief from the oppressive heat.

Audrey watched from the corner of her eye as her daughter tucked the crocheted afghan around her thin legs. Though it was scorching hot outside, the temperature was pleasant in the house. There was certainly no need for a blanket. But Leslie was always cold. It was no wonder, thought her mother. There wasn't any flesh on those bones.

As Audrey had feared, the story after the first commercial break was about her daughter, the girl who authorities claimed had faked her own abduction and forced the entire shore town into a frenzied three-day search.

Leslie whispered at the TV screen, "It wasn't the entire town. Shawn Ostrander didn't bother to look for me at all."

Audrey went to take her daughter's hand, but Leslie pulled away. "Don't bother, Mom. You can't make it all right. Just leave me alone."

Together, they watched the rest of the local news in

silence. As the news anchors were thanking their audience and saying good-bye, the phone rang. Audrey's brow wrinkled with concern as she looked over at her daughter.

"It's probably another one of those reporters." Audrey sighed. "Why can't they leave us alone?"

"I'll get it," Leslie said and began to get up from the couch. A bit too eagerly, thought Audrey.

"No," she said quickly, gently pulling her daughter back. "It's better if I handle it." Picking up the receiver, Audrey heard a female voice.

"Hello. This is Diane Mayfield from KEY News. Am I speaking with Mrs. Patterson?"

"Yes." Audrey held back from executing her original plan to shut down immediately any request for comment. This wasn't some local news reporter. This was the national news calling. Audrey was a regular *Hourglass* viewer and admired Diane Mayfield. Diane had a nice way about her, getting the information she wanted by coaxing her subjects to open up, not hammering at them. Not like some reporters. The ones who were sharks going in for the kill.

CHAPTER 10

Matthew Voigt sat in Diane's office, listening to her side of the phone conversation and occasionally mouthing suggestions. As Diane put down the receiver, he leaned forward. "Well? What did she say?"

Diane shrugged. "At least she didn't say no. She said she'd think about it."

"And?"

"She's seen me on *Hourglass* and says she admires my work."

"Good. That should help us." Matthew sat back. "You can bet we aren't the only ones who want to interview Leslie Patterson. If her mother likes you, it increases our chances of getting a shot with her daughter."

"Okay," said Diane as she stood up and walked to the front of her desk. "That's about all we can do from here. When are you leaving for Ocean Grove?"

"I'm stopping home to pack a bag, and then I'll head right down," Matthew said. "I'll be there later this afternoon and try to get some elements lined up. I'll see you there in the morning."

Diane nodded. "Who's our crew?" she asked.

"Gates and Bing."

Diane rolled her eyes. "Great. Just great."

"Believe me, I'm sorry too, Diane. I tried for Cohen and Doyle, but they're on vacation. We're stuck with Sammy."

"God, Matthew. The last time Sammy Gates shot my stand-up, I looked like a hag. He didn't bother telling me that my hair was sticking up in the back, and it was as if he was actually trying to enlarge the dark circles under my eyes. The guy doesn't even make an effort to set up the lighting gear properly."

Matthew nodded. "I know. But I promise, I'll be all over him, Diane. I'll make sure Sammy makes you look good."

She knew Matthew would be true to his word. Of all the talented *Hourglass* segment producers, Matthew was her favorite. He was meticulous in his researching and planning, yet able to fly by his wits when the situation called for it. There was no such thing as a predictable shoot, and Matthew Voigt was skilled at understanding what needed to be done in a changing situation. Each of the *Hourglass* correspondents had a list of which producers they preferred to work with. Matthew was on everyone's roster.

"Okay, if you say so. I'll be counting on you." Diane glanced at her watch. "So, I'm going to go downstairs, grab something to eat at my desk, and finish some paperwork I had planned to get done before leaving for the vacation I'm not taking. Then I'll go home to pack and face the firing squad."

CHAPTER 11

Shawn started to pull out his sunglasses but thought better of it. He knew from experience that Arthur didn't trust anyone who covered his eyes.

His bartending job at the Stone Pony paid the bills, but the release of the mentally ill into the community had been Shawn's true focus all summer. He was working on his master's thesis, and Ocean Grove provided a good location for research, since at one point, the town had become a dumping ground for people released from downsizing New Jersey psychiatric hospitals. The town's old wooden hotels and boardinghouses were convenient places to deposit the mentally ill. Ocean Grove became known not only for having a large concentration of Victorian homes but for having one of the largest concentrations of discharged psychiatric patients in the United States.

Shawn had grown up watching the poor souls aimlessly walking the boardwalk, smoking cigarettes, and drinking coffee. Everyone complained that the state had made few provisions for their care once they were living in the outside world. No outpatient clinic was opened, no activity center or vocational training program was offered. Little effort was made to assure that the patients took their medication.

The state had given scant thought to the discharged people and none to the quality of life of the citizens who lived around them. Though Ocean Grove had a long tradition of tolerance and caring for the less fortunate, residents were beside themselves as incidents of shoplifting and indecent exposure infested their lovely seaside enclave. Owners of hotels and bed-and-breakfast inns saw their businesses decline, and Ocean Grove property values sharply decreased.

Finally, the townspeople organized and got legislation passed that limited the number of boardinghouses for discharged psychiatric patients. Residents were relocated in other communities around New Jersey with vows that, this time, more outpatient services and rehabilitation would be provided.

As he looked for Arthur, Shawn recalled the day that had influenced the rest of his life, the day he had watched a former mental patient commit suicide by jumping from the roof of a hotel in the center of town. For a ten-year-old boy, the sight had been scarring, fascinating, and formative. It had led an impressionable child to wonder about things he had never really considered before. Why were some people deranged and others weren't? Wasn't there something that could be done to help the ones who had been so unfairly afflicted? Wasn't it his responsibility to try?

His father hadn't been thrilled when Shawn told his parents he wanted to become a social worker, but his mother said she was proud she had raised a son who wanted to help others and contribute to making the world a better place. As an undergraduate at Monmouth University, Shawn had majored in social work. Next month he would go back to the New Brunswick campus of Rutgers University to continue working on his master's thesis. Today he was looking for Arthur Tomkins, released from the VA hospital, tormented by his memories of the Gulf War, and living in Ocean Grove.

Shawn scanned the boardwalk to the north, actually seeing waves of heat hovering over the planks. The pathway along the edge of the beach stretched all the way to the town limits, where Asbury Park's old, eerily beautiful Casino, a cavernous art deco building, stood in virtual ruins. The Casino, once the site of an ice-skating palace and carousel with hand-carved, gaily painted horses, now stood only as a reminder of the faded grandeur of Ocean Grove's next-door neighbor.

Arthur was nowhere to be seen. Shawn started walking toward the Casino, unable to keep from gazing at the ocean. The dark blue water teased him, tempting him to forget his research and run into the refreshing surf. His conscience made him keep going.

Shawn knew that Arthur had come to enjoy the time the two of them spent together. But when Shawn had brought Leslie along with him, and the other day, when he'd introduced Carly to Arthur, the poor guy had seemed to alternate between enthusiasm and sadness. Shawn could tell Arthur enjoyed meeting the young women, but there were times during the conversations when Arthur would shut down and stare out to the ocean. Shawn knew enough about Arthur's past to suspect that he was thinking about his old girlfriend who'd dumped him while he was in the service.

Just when he was ready to give up, Shawn spotted Arthur in his military fatigues coming around the side of the Casino, heading for the nearest boardwalk bench and circling it three times before sitting down.

Shawn picked up his pace, went directly to the bench, and took a seat beside Arthur. He noticed the man needed a shave and could use a haircut too.

"Hey, buddy. Where you been?" Shawn asked.

"Oh, you know, Shawn. Here and there."

"Been taking your meds, Arthur?" Shawn put his hand on Arthur's shoulder.

"Sure, Shawn." Arthur nodded three times. "You know I always do what you tell me to do."

CHAPTER 12

As he brought the couple and their baby back to their car, Larry Belcaro couldn't help but feel sorry for them. How were young people supposed to afford a place at the beach? The prices had gone through the roof. Though that was good for Surfside Realty and therefore good for him, Larry believed it wasn't all that good for the area in general. The Jersey Shore was meant to be a place where families could come to enjoy the ocean and one another. To his mind, those simple pleasures should be available to everyone, not only to those with hefty incomes.

As he was steering his beige sedan onto Webb Avenue, a memory flashed, uninvited, through Larry's mind. A little girl with dark, curly hair sitting under a brilliant blue sky, digging in the sand. A tiny nose and soft, white shoulders turning pink in the bright summer sun. A contented smile spreading across the face of his angel as she called to him to look at her castle.

Larry pulled to a stop in front of the salmon-colored turreted Victorian and shook his head, trying to clear the visions from his mind's eye. He never got used to them. Sometimes the memories came flooding back, catching him totally off guard, like now, after he'd been with a happy young family, a family just as his had once been. Sometimes the recollections were predictable in their arrival. They'd come when he'd hear someone talk of a kid's college graduation. They'd come at a wedding when the father of the bride danced with his daughter. They'd come at a niece's or nephew's christening party. Whenever a life event signaled something Larry had never had a chance to experience with Jenna, the memories haunted him.

How had it all gone so desperately wrong?

As he forced himself to get out of the car, Larry wondered why he even bothered asking himself that question anymore. It had been almost two years since Jenna had passed and a year since her mother had followed her. Larry had played and replayed it all in his mind, day after painful day, night after sleepless night. He always came up with the same answer. It was his fault.

He should have done more for Jenna, found better help for her. He shouldn't have been so trusting of that despicable charlatan who called himself a therapist. He should have insisted that Jenna stop seeing the quack when not only didn't they see any improvement but she actually seemed to be getting worse. But Jenna had begged to be able to keep going to her sessions with Owen Messinger. She was convinced that she needed him to get well. Finally, both her parents had given up, not knowing what else to do.

That was no excuse, Larry realized now. Sure, they had been desperate to have someone help Jenna, but they should have acted on their instincts. Deep inside they sensed that Owen Messinger was hurting, not helping, their daughter. They should have moved heaven and earth to make him stop. They could have quit paying his bills or moved away or even locked Jenna up for her own good. Anything to protect her from that evil man.

Instead, they'd been accomplices in her death. Twice a week Larry and his wife had driven their daughter to the appointments. He would never forgive himself for that. Jenna's mother was consumed by guilt too, and that, along with her broken heart, had led her to take her own life—in effect, anyway. Marie had been drinking way too much in the months after Jenna slit her wrists. Finally, one night in her inebriated state, she crashed her car into a telephone pole.

Now, it was just him.

Noticing the pink and white geraniums brimming from the flower boxes strapped to the railing that circled the front porch, Larry was fully aware there wasn't anything he could do to change all that had happened. But he was determined to do something that would help other people in the same tortured boat as his family had been. Around Easter time, he had taken the first step, when he'd followed a thin young woman as she came out of Owen Messinger's office, tailing her right to the house he stood in front of now.

For weeks, he'd repeatedly driven by the house, catching sight of Leslie from time to time as she entered or, better yet, when she exited. He'd tailed her, and when the time was right, he'd seen her going into Lavender & Lace. He'd followed her inside and acted like a customer. He'd struck up a conversation with Leslie and her mother and mentioned that he was looking for help at his office. Now, Leslie worked for him and he could watch out for her.

Audrey Patterson answered the door. "It's so good of you to come, Larry. You've been a wonderful boss to Leslie, and a good friend as well."

After leading Larry into the living room to see her daughter, Audrey went to the kitchen to fix some lemonade. Larry turned to the young woman and spoke gently.

"I'm so glad you're all right, Leslie," he said, sincerity in his eyes as well as his voice.

"But no one believes me, Larry," Leslie said. "Someone took me and held me against my will. Why doesn't anyone believe me?"

"It doesn't matter what they think, Leslie. It only matters that you take care of yourself and get well. Nothing is more important than that."

As tears welled in Leslie's brown eyes, Larry was reminded again of his own daughter. He was fiercely determined to make amends.

"Do you believe me, Larry?" Leslie sniffed. "Please, tell me you believe me."

"I believe you have been through a terrible ordeal, Leslie. I also believe that probably the very best thing you could do for yourself is get back to work. Get your mind off everything. Take the weekend to rest. But I want you to know, your job is waiting for you. Please come back to the office on Monday morning, Leslie. It's always been my experience that work is the best therapy."

CHAPTER 13

What should have taken him just over an hour had taken him two and a half in the late Friday afternoon traffic on the Garden State Parkway. When he finally reached Ocean Grove, Jonathan had to spend another half hour looking for a parking space. By the time he found one, unloaded his gear, and walked the six hot blocks to their tent, he was smoldering, physically and mentally.

When he opened the screen door, there was no one inside the tent. Jonathan wasn't sure if he was annoyed or relieved. Was it too much to ask that after he'd sat in that miserable traffic for so long his family be there to greet him? With disgust he walked the few feet back into the cabin portion of their tiny summer home and tossed his duffel bag down on the meticulously made-up double bed.

On the other hand, it was nice to have some time to himself, because for the next week, he knew he would have virtually no privacy at all. He and Helen and the kids would be tripping all over one another. And he should probably forget about having any intimate time alone with his wife. Helen would be worried that the children or the neighbors would hear any sound they might make. That was another reason Jonathan hated tent living.

But Helen loved it, and the girls always seemed so happy and healthy down here. What kind of a husband and father would he be if he deprived his family of storybook summers like these?

Another few steps took him into the minuscule kitchen area. He went to the junior-size refrigerator, took out a can of Coke, and guzzled it down. It wasn't the icy beer he craved, but it would have to do. Alcoholic beverages were not sold in Ocean Grove. Jonathan knew better than to bring a case down with him. Helen wouldn't hear of having it in the tent. That was just the way it was.

At least he had gotten her to agree to hire a babysitter and get out tonight. Last year they'd found a dance place that served drinks in Bradley Beach. Their tenth anniversary was coming up soon, and it would be great for them to get out alone together for the evening. They needed to reconnect, and he needed to blow off some steam. There were too many pretty girls with lean, young bodies working in his office, and he'd been finding himself admiring them a bit too much this summer.

CHAPTER 14

Table conversation at the Mayfield home was a mix of Diane and Emily's trying to paint a bright face on the changed vacation plans, Anthony's vociferously expressing his displeasure, and Michelle's sitting in sullen silence as she pushed around the spaghetti on her dinner plate.

"Look. It's not like you guys are being asked to go to boot camp or something," Diane said. "Do you have any idea how many kids would do anything to have a vacation at the beach?"

"Ah, Mom, give it up, will you?" Anthony shook his head. "Going to the beach is okay, but we've gone to Amagansett lots of other summers. Been there, done that. I told my friends I was going to the Grand Canyon, and now I'll seem like such a dork. If you ask me, the Jersey Shore doesn't even come close to the Grand Canyon."

Diane's patience was wearing thin. "You know what, Anthony? I am sorry we aren't going on the trip we were planning on. I really am, honey. But if I want to keep my job at KEY News, I have to take this assignment. That's all there is to it. You just have to understand." She paused, concerned that what she was tempted to say next would wound her son. But she decided to go ahead. Father in jail or not, her son needed to get it straight. "And to tell you the truth, Anthony, you sound like a spoiled brat."

Now Anthony joined his sister, staring at his plate in silence.

"More garlic bread, anybody?" Emily asked, trying to break the heavy mood. As the bread basket went around the table, Diane noted that her daughter passed on it while the three others at the table each took another piece.

"Michelle, Emily's garlic bread is delicious." Diane held the basket out again to her daughter. "Why don't you have some, sweetheart?"

"Because I've already had two pieces, Mom." Michelle didn't bother keeping the exasperation out of her voice.

Diane was ready to put her daughter in her place for the snippy response, but she knew that if she came down too hard, Michelle would only storm off and leave the rest of her dinner uneaten. Lately it seemed the fourteen-year-old was almost looking for a reason to get angry. Diane had been chalking it up as a reaction to the stress and embarrassment caused by knowing that her father was in jail along with a predictable case of teenage rebellion. But despite the many conversations she had had with her daughter, things were not getting better.

Deciding to ignore Michelle's comment, Diane plowed ahead, describing the advantages of their new trip. "Look. There's the beach every day. We can go to the movies or play miniature golf at night. There must be rides on the boardwalk somewhere nearby, so we can do that. Maybe there will be a concert you guys would want to see. Anthony, after dinner, why don't you see what you can find out on the Internet?"

At that, Anthony lifted his digital camera, held it steady with both hands, framed his mother in the light display, and pressed down on the shutter release. The camera's flash blinded Diane.

"Anthony!" Diane yelled, exasperated. "I've told you a million times not to bring that thing to the table. Daddy and I wanted you to have the camera as a positive influence, but you're getting to be so annoying with it. If you bring it to the table one more time, you can take a picture of me killing you!"

The rest of the dinner conversation consisted of Diane and Emily talking over what still needed to be done before the family left for Ocean Grove in the morning.

"May I be excused, please?" asked Michelle, and Diane felt a moment of relief. All traces of politeness were not entirely gone. There was hope.

"Yes. Go ahead."

"Me too?"

"Yes, Anthony. You too."

Both siblings took their plates into the kitchen. Michelle scraped hers into the trash can, and Anthony left his on the counter next to the sink.

"You did the cooking, Em. I'll clean up," Diane volunteered.

"No argument from me." Emily grinned. "I'm going to run out to the drugstore and get some sunscreen and lip balm. Want anything?"

"A large bottle of Advil would probably be a good idea."

"Done."

Diane heard the front door of the apartment click closed as she took Anthony's plate and napkin from the countertop and pushed her foot down on the trash can pedal. She was about to scrape the pasta left on the plate into the garbage when her eyes fell on the contents already in the can. Two pieces of untouched garlic bread lay on top of Michelle's paper napkin.

CHAPTER 15

"Diane Mayfield from KEY News called today, Lou. She wants to interview Leslie."

Leslie stood near the door, with her back against the dining room wall, straining to hear her parents' low conversation on the other side. Audrey and Lou Patterson were at the kitchen table, sipping decaffeinated tea and trying to decide what to do to unravel their daughter's mess.

"I don't think we should commit to anything, Audrey—not until we have an attorney who can tell us what Leslie will be facing if the police decide they can prove she faked the whole thing." It was her father's deep voice. "I've gotten a few names. One's local, and the other two are big shots from Hudson County. Which way do you think we should go, Aud? Go with the guy who knows the area and the Neptune police, or go for the best representation money can buy?"

"I want both." It was her mother's voice. "Can't we have both?"

"You mean hire the local lawyer as well as one from up north?" Leslie surmised that her mother must have nodded her assent, because her father spoke again. "Not unless we suddenly win the lottery, Aud. We don't have that kind of money. You know that, honey."

As she heard her mother start to cry, Leslie could picture her father reaching out to take hold of his wife's arm, trying to reassure her. "It's gonna be all right, Aud. I promise."

"No. It's not going to be all right, Lou." Her mother's voice grew louder now. "It hasn't been all right for years, and it's not suddenly going to be all right now. All I know is I am not going to have my only child punished because she isn't well. That's really what this amounts to. Leslie is mentally unstable, and that's why she pulled this stunt. Any defense lawyer worth his salt should be able to prove that. We can show that she's been in one kind of therapy or another for years."

"I'm afraid the police don't consider this a mere stunt, Audrey. And people around town don't either.

Some folks may feel sorry for Leslie, but they don't want to set a precedent by letting her off with a slap on the wrist. It cost a bundle to have all that searching done, and people don't appreciate having their time and tax dollars wasted. They don't want to get stuck footing the bill for the next girl who decides to cry wolf to get some attention. They'll want to set an example with our daughter."

Leslie could feel her pulse race as her cheeks grew hot. She had sensed the police didn't believe her story, but it hadn't occurred to her that her parents didn't believe her either, or that she could possibly go to jail. She had heard lots of stories about what happened in prison, and the idea terrified her. Leslie couldn't control the deep sob that forced its way up through her throat.

"Leslie? Is that you, honey?" Audrey got up from the table and went through the door, finding her daughter crouched and hugging herself in the darkened dining room.

"Oh, Leslie. Come here, sweetheart." Audrey wrapped her arms around the young woman and urged her to stand up. "It will be all right, Leslie, you'll see. Come in with Daddy and me and we'll talk."

"I don't want to talk," Leslie wailed. "I don't want to go to jail. I didn't do anything wrong, Mom. I swear I didn't."

"Shh, Leslie. It's all right. You aren't going to jail, honey." Audrey held her sobbing daughter as Lou came into the dining room and turned on the light.

"Tell Leslie it's going to be all right, Lou."

"We're going to get the best lawyer, Leslie. Don't you worry," her father answered, unable to attest to something he wasn't sure was true. "He'll know how to handle this. He'll be able to straighten everything out."

Leslie could not be consoled. She continued sobbing, not only at the idea of the punishment she could face but also letting out the tension and hurt she had been feeling all day. It was bad enough Shawn hadn't looked for her when she was missing; he hadn't even bothered coming to see her today to tell her he was glad she was alive.

CHAPTER 16

Thank God, Helen had agreed to get out of Ocean Grove and drive south to Bradley Beach, where they could let loose a little bit. A nice lobster dinner and a couple of beers made Jonathan feel much better. Afterward, as he and Helen danced to the strains of the Motown music, he found himself actually having a good time. This was the way it should be. This was normal adult life at the beach. A few drinks and some loud music and some fun. Not tee-totaling and mind-numbing quiet after 10:00 P.M., or reading Bible passages before lights out, with nothing to look forward to but more of the same the next day.

But Jonathan's pleasure faded as he saw his wife look at her watch. "Come on, Helen. It's early," he groaned.

"It's almost ten-thirty. By the time we get home it'll be eleven."

"You've got to be kidding."

"The kids will be up early in the morning, Jonathan."

"So what? They can watch cartoons while we sleep a little more."

"We don't have television down here, remember?"

Jonathan smiled slyly. "I brought a portable with me. It's in the trunk."

She knew better than to fight with him. Helen had learned to pick her battles and ultimately win the war. She agreed to a few more dances, knowing full well that a television set would come into their tent over her dead body.

CHAPTER 17

As she walked down the hallway to get ready for bed, Diane heard the shower running. Michelle had left the door to her bedroom ajar, and Diane walked inside. A duffel bag lay on the floor, stuffed with enough clothes for an entire summer. The miniature DVD player Michelle had begged for as a Christmas present along with a stack of movies were piled next to the bag.

Another canvas bag was filled with a boom box, Walkman, and CDs.

Demanding that her teenage daughter pack more economically wasn't worth the effort. Diane knew that. The other mothers she traded notes with reported exactly the same thing. The day would come when Michelle would want to simplify and carry as little as possible on a trip, but that day wasn't going to be for a while. Now her daughter felt it was necessary to bring everything she might possibly need or want with her.

Picking up the teen magazine that lay open on Michelle's bed, Diane began flipping through it. Between the articles on boyfriends and acne were pages of advertisements for jeans and shoes and hand-bags and makeup. As the shoes were danced in and the jeans swaggered in, there was no ignoring it. Every single one of the female models that the companies used to sell their products was thin. In some cases, almost impossibly thin.

Diane looked up to see her daughter standing in the doorway. There was a white towel twisted around her head and a larger, longer one wrapped around her body. Was she imagining it, or did Michelle's shoulders look bonier than the last time she had seen them? Diane tried to think back. They hadn't been at the beach or at a pool together all summer. When Diane came home from work in the evenings, Michelle usually had on a cotton T-shirt. Come to think of it, she'd been wearing ones with long sleeves, always complaining that the apartment air-conditioning was too cold. Diane hadn't thought anything of it, until now.

CHAPTER 18

It was a real drag that the Richeys didn't have a television set. But since this wasn't the first time Carly had babysat for them, she had known enough to bring her Walkman and some magazines. Hannah and Sarah had been worn out from the heat and a long day at the beach and had conked out only an hour after their parents left. They were sound asleep now in their bunk beds pushed against the canvas wall.

Carly got up from the wicker chair and wandered into the kitchen, stopping to adjust the air conditioner. There was no way she would have taken this job tonight if the Richeys hadn't had air-conditioning. She could live without TV for a couple of hours, but she wasn't into sweating. But even cranked up as high as it could go, the air conditioner was fighting a losing battle against a heat wave that just wouldn't quit.

Carly pulled open the fridge and rifled through the contents. She spied some ice pops wedged on top of the ice cube tray in the tiny freezer section and selected an orange one. *Lots of bang for the caloric buck,* she thought as she pulled off the paper wrapper. And all water, nothing to bloat her. Carly patted her stomach to make sure it was still as flat as it had been the last time she checked, about an hour ago.

She wanted to look great for Shawn when she met him at the Stone Pony later. He wasn't the best looking guy she had ever dated, but there was something about him that really appealed to her. Shawn had the sweetest way about him. He actually listened when she talked—not like other guys, who were more concerned with what *they* had to say than what was on her mind. Carly really liked Shawn, and she could tell he felt the same about her.

Another thing she appreciated about Shawn was the fact that he didn't make her uncomfortable. He didn't leer at her, making her feel so uneasy. Not the way Mr. Richey had when she'd arrived tonight.

The only thing that bothered her about Shawn was the fact that he hadn't looked for Leslie Patterson. Just because they'd broken up didn't mean he shouldn't be concerned about what happened to his old girlfriend.

Going back to the front of the tent, Carly curled up in the wicker chair and opened the new issue of *InStyle*. She was engrossed in the pictures of Cameron Diaz's lean legs when she heard the screen door creak.

"It's me, Carly." Helen Richey whispered the announcement as she tiptoed into the tent. "We're home."

The mother went directly to look at her sleeping girls. "How were they?" she asked softly as she gently pulled the thumb from her younger child's mouth.

"Fine. They were great, Mrs. Richey. We played a

couple of rounds of Candy Land, and then they actually asked to go to bed." Carly looked at the screen door again. "Where's Mr. Richey?"

"He's looking for a parking space. He dropped me off." Helen continued tucking in the cotton blankets on the bunk beds.

Carly began to gather up her paraphernalia. "Okay, Mrs. Richey. I guess I'll be going then. Call me again whenever you need me."

"Oh no, Carly." Helen straightened up from her bent position and went to open her purse. "You have to wait for Jonathan. I want him to walk you home." She pressed the folded bills into Carly's hand. "Thank you so much," she said.

The thought of walking alone with Mr. Richey creeped Carly out. "That's okay, Mrs. Richey. Really. It's such a short walk. I'm fine going by myself."

Before Helen Richey could utter another word, the babysitter bolted out of the tent.

Jonathan found a place to park right around the corner from the tent, but he took his time getting out of the car. He was in no rush. The thought of going back to the tent made him claustrophobic.

He stared out the windshield trying to summon up his resolve. He was going to break the news to Helen tomorrow. This would absolutely be the last summer vacation he would spend in the tent. If his wife wanted all of them to be together next year, they should spend this week looking for a real house down here.

He opened the car door and got out but decided not to go to the trunk and get the portable TV. There would be time enough tomorrow to have a fight. No sense having one tonight—not that they could have anyway, considering how everyone lived cheek by jowl in these damned tents.

As he was about to come to the corner to make the turn onto Bath Avenue, he saw a figure sprint across the street in the moonlight. It was Carly, her blond hair flowing behind her. He had forgotten he was supposed to walk her home. It would have been nice to have a little harmless fantasy, getting to spend a few minutes alone with her.

Jonathan was about to call out to her but thought better of it. Instead he just followed her.

CHAPTER 19

The bath didn't help. Neither did the cup of herbal tea. Diane just couldn't fall asleep. She lay alone in the darkness and wished that tonight, more than any night since he'd gone, Philip was lying beside her.

She turned over and pulled the pillow from his side of the bed, holding it close.

Visions spun through Diane's mind, things she hadn't thought much of when she noticed them. Michelle's recent preoccupation with exercise, her insistence that she get her run in every day, along with making sure she followed the instructions on that exercise video she always seemed to be playing. Diane had written it off as simply a teenage girl becoming more aware of her figure.

The container of ice cream that had been sitting, unopened, in the freezer for months. Ben & Jerry's Chunky Monkey, Michelle's favorite. For years Michelle had requested it every time Diane went for groceries. Again, she hadn't been concerned, knowing that what a kid loved wasn't always what a teenager preferred.

Diane hugged the pillow closer as she thought of Michelle's garlic bread in the trash and tried to recall her daughter's eating habits of late. There hadn't been enough family meals since Philip went to prison. Many evenings she'd gotten home from work and Emily and the kids said they'd already eaten. Truth be known, Diane guiltily admitted to herself, she'd been relieved on lots of those nights. It was easier to pour a bowl of cereal or scramble a couple of eggs for herself and eat in solitude with a magazine, not having to expend the energy to engage in conversation. The stress of having her husband away in such disgrace along with the pressures at the office left Diane wrung out at night.

Though she had been making it a point to avoid speaking engagements, dinner plans, and anything else that would keep her from being at home with the kids in the evening, Diane mentally berated herself. Being there physically didn't mean she'd always been there emotionally. She realized now that perhaps she had been so wrapped up in her own heartache and worry, she hadn't been paying enough attention to her daughter's.

But she had damn well better start paying attention now. Diane punched the pillow resolutely. If this was the start of an eating disorder, it had to be dealt with immediately and decisively. It would affect Michelle's health and could lead to even more destructive behaviors. Look at Leslie Patterson. How ironic that just this morning she had been feeling sorry for the Patterson family when Diane could be facing the same problem herself.

Thank God, Michelle wasn't cutting herself too, or at least Diane didn't think she was. Her heart beat faster at the thought. She wondered what had come first for Leslie Patterson. Did the cutting follow the eating disorder or vice versa? Did the two destructive behaviors go hand in hand? Diane squeezed her eyes shut tighter and concentrated.

Dear Lord, please help me nip this in the bud.

She felt a bit of ease as she silently prayed, but in the back of her mind, she knew that asking for God's help was only part of the solution. Diane was going to have to stay on top of this.

CHAPTER 20

Carly searched the dimly lit room until she spotted Shawn behind the bar. The slender blonde maneuvered her way through the crowd and slid onto an empty stool. Shawn's face lit up when he saw her.

"I thought you'd never get here." He leaned over the bar and spoke loudly into her ear to be heard over the band.

"Me, neither," Carly shouted back.

"What'll you have?" he asked.

"A Coke, I guess," she answered glumly. "Unless you feel like surprising me."

Shawn made no comment. He knew Carly wasn't of legal drinking age. She was old enough to drive a car and vote and even serve in the armed forces. But she wasn't legally allowed to have an alcoholic drink in New Jersey. It didn't make much sense.

He partially filled her glass with Coke and quickly splashed in some rum. If the boss found out he was mixing a drink for someone underage, he would be out of a job so fast it would make his head spin. But the boss wasn't around right now, and it wouldn't hurt Carly to have a drink or two.

"Do you think you should take it a little bit easier, Carly?" Shawn asked as he watched her suck the contents of a second drink through a straw. "At least just take sips."

"Don't worry about me, Shawn," she said with a smile. "I can hold my liquor. Hey, do you ever get a break? Do you think we can get in a dance?"

Even in the crowded room, she stands out. She's pretty and animated and looks happy. And what a dancer! She gyrates to the beat of the music as though she's been doing it all her life. She's so obviously enjoying herself.

It's good that she's so petite. It'll make things much easier.

The music stopped. Carly and Shawn went back to the bar while the band took a break.

"How was the babysitting?" he asked in an even voice, now that they didn't have to yell to each other to be heard.

"Oh, fine. The kids are really cute, and Mrs. Richey pays well. But that Mr. Richey . . ."

"What?" Shawn encouraged her to continue.

"I don't know. He doesn't exactly fit the 'tent' mold. I mean, I don't think he's too happy about being there." Carly decided not to mention the way Mr. Richey looked at her. She wasn't sure yet if Shawn was the jealous type. She decided to change the subject. "Have you heard anything more about Leslie?" she asked.

"Oh, God, Carly. Let's not ruin the night talking about Leslie." He groaned.

"I'd have thought you would care more about her,

Shawn. You went out with her for a long time." Carly tried to stifle a hiccup.

"Look, Carly. It's over with Leslie. That's it. *Finito.* I don't want to talk about it. I thought you got that."

The liquor was working its wonders on her now. Carly didn't like the impatient tone of Shawn's voice, and she wasn't going to let things lie. "Well, I'd hope that someday, if we've been going out for a long time and I disappeared, you would give a damn," she sulked.

"Well, *I* would hope that you wouldn't be crazy enough to run away and hide and pretend you were kidnapped," Shawn shot back. He turned to fill an order called from the other end of the bar.

Trouble in paradise. She doesn't look so happy anymore.

Just an hour ago, who knew how things would turn out? Such a simple plan: find a girl to dance with— and keep hidden until she's served her purpose. Now that she's leaving, heading for the exit, plans need to change.

Carly heard the low roar of the ocean as she crossed the street. She turned right, heading south toward Ocean Grove. She could walk home from the Stone Pony in less than ten minutes.

The night air was warm but fresh and salty, and it sobered her somewhat. How had everything gone wrong so quickly with Shawn just now? Had she overreacted? Was he really a jerk and not the nice guy she had thought him to be?

She walked along the curb, watching out for pieces of glass that could cut through the thin soles of her sandals. The streets in Asbury Park weren't as clean as Ocean Grove's. Nothing about Asbury Park was the same as Ocean Grove. Fronting the Atlantic Ocean was the only thing they shared.

As she approached the border between the two towns, she could see the old brick Casino silhouetted against the night sky. The once grand building had been deserted for years. In the light cast by a solitary streetlamp, Carly could make out the DANGER: KEEP OUT sign.

She paused for a minute as she decided how to proceed. She could walk all the way around Wesley Lake or just follow the narrow pathway that edged around the Casino, then cut across the few yards of sand that led to the beginning of the Ocean Grove boardwalk. Her house was just a couple of blocks from there.

Though it was dark and she was a bit wobbly on her feet, she opted for the familiar pathway, the one she had played on so many times as a kid. She kept her left arm extended, her hand touching the Casino's outer wall as she followed the rounded contour of the building. It was just as she was about to jump down from the pathway to the sand that a gloved hand slammed an old brick down on her head.

SATURDAY
AUGUST 20

CHAPTER 21

The promise of the sun's arrival was signaled on the ocean's horizon. The light was changing, ever so slowly, the inky black sky fading to dark gray. As he stepped onto the boardwalk, Arthur knew the grayness would gradually get lighter and lighter until the sun's orange and yellow rays took over and finally lit up the azure sky over the dark blue sea.

It was basically the same every day. Arthur knew because he never slept well. He was usually out on the boardwalk by 4:00 A.M. It was his favorite time of day, before the joggers came or the fishermen arrived to cast their lines in the water. At this precious hour he had the boardwalk to himself.

Since he came to live in Ocean Grove after he'd been released from the VA hospital, there wasn't a morning gone by, a stroll down the boardwalk taken, that Arthur hadn't thought of Bonnie. The first time he saw the water every day, heard a seagull's early cry, and listened to the never-ending rumble of the ocean, he thought of her. Today was no different.

A welcome breeze swept in from the ocean, blowing Arthur's partially unbuttoned three-color desert camouflage shirt open. A rare gift of late, the gust felt good against his face and chest. Arthur enjoyed it, dreading the unremitting heat that was coming again later today.

A blue-and-white Dodge Durango stopped at the curb alongside his spot on the boardwalk. "How ya doin', Art?" the overnight police officer called over the strip of grass that separated the two men.

"I'm doing all right. How 'bout yourself?" Arthur said amiably, concealing his disappointment that no matter how many times he asked the cops to call him Arthur, they continued to address him as Art.

"Fine, Art. Thanks for asking," said the cop. "Been out here long, Art?"

"No. I just got here."

"See anything out of the ordinary?" the policeman asked.

"Like what?"

"We got a call from the parents of one of the local girls saying she hasn't come home since she left for a babysitting job last night."

Arthur felt himself growing anxious. "Well, I didn't see any girl," he answered quickly, before coughing three times.

"Nobody's saying you did, Art. But if you do see anything, let us know, will you? We're looking for a blond girl, about five-foot-one, thin, pretty. In fact, she's a waitress at Nagle's. Carly Neath. Know her?"

Filled with trepidation, Arthur tried to decide how to answer. Yes, he knew her. Shawn had brought Carly with him one time when he came out on the boardwalk to talk. But Arthur was afraid to tell the cop about that. If the police thought he knew Carly, they might think he had something to do with her not coming home last night. People like him were always among the first suspected when anything went wrong.

"Nope. Don't know her."

Arthur kept walking on the boards that hovered over the beach as the police car followed slowly alongside for a while and then pulled away. Arthur thought about the pretty girl who had smiled so brightly when Shawn had introduced her that day. She'd reminded him a lot of Bonnie.

When he reached his favorite bench, he circled it three times before taking a seat. Uncontrollably, Arthur's mind segued from thoughts of Shawn's girlfriend to Bonnie, calling up the memories, still surprisingly clear, despite the time gone by and the medication designed to take the edge off his pain. The medicine, when he took it, did the job, somewhat. Though Arthur didn't get as agitated as he used to when he thought of Bonnie, nothing could eradicate her from his mind. And though he still harbored some anger toward her for what she'd done to him, to them, that didn't mean he would ever want to forget her.

She had been his first love and his only love. Arthur knew he could never love someone again the way he'd loved Bonnie. He also knew that someone like Bonnie was never going to love him. Not the way he was now. Who was going to love a man without a job, a guy living on the government dole? Who was going to love a man who spent his nights on a lumpy mattress in a boardinghouse and his days drinking coffee and wandering around town?

Arthur pulled a package from his breast pocket and shook out a cigarette. Striking a match, he lit up and inhaled deeply, peering down to the end of the board-walk, where the old Casino was framed against the now dove-gray sky. He let out a long stream of smoke through his nostrils and let his mind wander farther down the torture trail.

What great times they'd had together. He pictured her petite figure swirling around on the dance floor, her pretty face beaming up at him. He remembered the way they'd laughed at the comedy clubs she loved to go to, the way they'd cheered and hugged each other at those Yankees games. He still remembered the fun they'd had picking out names for the children they were going to have someday, after they got married, after he finished his stint with the Army.

Arthur rose from the bench and, with an angry flick, threw his cigarette out onto the beach. Bonnie had promised that she would be waiting for him when he got back from Desert Storm. Bonnie had lied.

CHAPTER 22

"Mom," Anthony whined as they stood in the small lobby of the Dancing Dunes Inn. "You have *got* to be kidding."

Diane had a sinking feeling as she scanned the space. A sleeping cat lay curled up on a spindle-legged bench, the only piece of furniture in the room. The wallpaper featured seagulls and sandpipers, faded, she suspected, from blue at one time to almost white now. The beige cotton curtains at the windows had been washed many times, to the point that they were almost sheers. The gray paint on the wooden floor was scuffed bare in spots. The lobby was devoid of color, but at least, Diane consoled herself, it seemed clean.

"All right, so it's not the Ritz," she whispered to her son. "But quit complaining right now. I mean it, Anthony."

Diane stole a look at Emily, who rolled her eyes at her older sister.

"May I help you?" A good-looking Latino man had taken his place behind the tiny registration desk. He wore a pale green oxford shirt with the sleeves carefully rolled up, exposing tanned and toned forearms. Diane judged him to be in his early thirties.

"Yes, thank you. I'm Diane Mayfield. We have some rooms reserved?"

"Ah yes, of course." The man smiled, exposing a set of even, dazzling white teeth. "You are with KEY News, right?"

Diane nodded.

"I'm sorry I wasn't right out here to meet you. I was in the back working at my computer on brochures for the inn. And I hope you can excuse the decor—or lack thereof," he apologized, gesturing outward as Diane noticed the gold band on his left hand. "My partner and I have just bought this place. We have big plans for it. But the renovations won't begin down here until after the summer season."

Diane searched for something tactful to say as she looked around the plain lobby. "Well, I'm sure it will be beautiful."

"I know it's not what you must be used to, Ms. Mayfield, but if there is anything we can do to make you and your family's stay here more comfortable, believe me, we will be all too happy to oblige. My name is Carlos. Carlos Hernandez." He reached out across the desk to shake Diane's hand.

"Nice to meet you, Carlos. This is my sister, Emily Abbott, and this is my son, Anthony. My daughter, Michelle, is getting her things from the car."

Carlos acknowledged his guests and then turned to the Peg-Board behind the desk. "Three rooms, right?" he asked as he reached for the keys that hung from the hooks.

"Actually, there should be four."

Carlos frowned as he checked his registry. "Well, we

do have four rooms booked for KEY News here, but one has already been taken by Mr. Gates."

"Sammy Gates?" Diane asked.

"Yes. Samuel Gates."

"Is Matthew Voigt registered?"

Carlos consulted his book again. "No. Just Mr. Gates."

Diane shrugged. "Well, that still doesn't explain why we don't have a fourth room for ourselves."

"Gee, I'm sorry, Ms. Mayfield. I wish we had another room for you, but we don't. Everything is booked solid at this time of year. As it is, we've reopened the top floor to accommodate you. We had been working up there to have some really nice rooms ready for the fall."

Diane looked at him with alarm.

"Don't worry," he reassured her. "It's not a disaster area up there. Kip and I worked all night getting things ready for you. We really are hoping to draw in people from the city, and we consider this a big opportunity. We want you to be satisfied."

As they entered the first room, Diane was charmed. The walls were painted a pale lemon yellow with bright white gloss on the baseboard and window trim. Twin brass beds were well polished and covered with clean, white, hand-crocheted spreads. A blue knotted rug decorated with garlands of yellow and white summer flowers covered the middle of the waxed pine floor. A series of botanical prints matted in blue and framed in white had been artfully hung. There were candles on the Victorian-style oak dresser, and a small pile of books and magazines were stacked on the bottom shelf of the night table between the beds.

"I call this room."

Diane turned to see Michelle in the doorway. She tried to keep her eyes trained on her daughter's face rather than on her body.

"Somebody's going to have to double up, honey."

"Not me. C'mon, Mom. I want my own room." Michelle walked over to the window and pulled back the eyelet curtain. "Look. This one has a great view of the beach." There was more enthusiasm in her daughter's voice than Diane had heard in a long while.

Diane looked at Emily while figuring out the arrangements in her head. Anthony should have a room to himself. That left two rooms for the three females. But would it be better if Michelle wasn't left alone?

"What do you think, Em?"

"I don't mind sharing, if you don't."

"All right," Diane decided. "We won't be in the rooms that much anyway. You can have this one, Michelle."

Carlos beckoned to them to follow him across the hall. "Well, then, that decides who will get the other rooms. There's a double bed in the Nautical Room and twin beds in the Shell Room. So, Anthony, this is your room."

Again, Diane was pleased. Pale blue walls, white trim, a fresh navy bedspread on the knobbed pine bed.

The prints on these walls displayed sailing vessels, and a sisal rug covered the floor.

Anthony nodded, grudging but approving as he tried out the mattress. "Not bad."

"Okay then. On to the Shell Room." Carlos led them down the hallway, stopping at a small doorway. "Here's the bathroom."

"*The* bathroom? As in the *only* bathroom?" Michelle asked with alarm. Carlos nodded.

"It's not the end of the world, Michelle, if we have to share a bathroom," Diane said, trying to keep the annoyance from her tone.

"I'm sorry there's only one bathroom up here," Carlos apologized. "We plan to put in another one, but for now there are plenty of clean towels, and we will collect and replace them every day."

"It's no problem at all, Carlos," Diane said, refraining from giving Michelle the withering glance she felt her daughter deserved. "This will be just fine."

A few minutes later, Diane and Emily were dividing up the drawers and unpacking their things. "Smell this sachet," Diane said as she held up the silk pouch she had pulled from the dresser drawer. "They've thought of everything, haven't they?"

Emily laughed. "What do you expect, Di?"

"What do you mean?"

"Duh. Carlos and his partner are gay."

Diane shrugged her shoulders as she replaced the sachet in the drawer. "Well, they sure know how to put the charm into a hotel."

CHAPTER 23

Helen had finished making up the beds and was in the kitchen stacking the breakfast dishes in the sink when she heard three raps on the front door frame. She pulled a tea towel from the rack, wiping her hands and wondering if Jonathan and the girls were back so soon from their walk into town to buy a newspaper. Why didn't they just come in? Opening the wooden door, she was greeted by a blast of hot air and two uniformed police officers, who stood on the narrow porch.

"Mrs. Richey?"

"Yes. Is something wrong?"

"We'd like to ask you a few questions, ma'am."

Helen noticed the sheen of perspiration on the fore-heads of both policemen. "Would you like to come inside, where it's cooler?" she asked.

"Thank you, ma'am. We would."

One man was a good five or six inches taller than the other, but both were broad-shouldered and solidly built. Their looming presence crowded the small front room of the tent.

"Please, sit down." Helen indicated the wicker chairs. "Would you like something to drink? I have lemonade all made."

"No thank you, ma'am," said the taller one.

Helen took a seat on the edge of the bottom bunk

bed and looked across the room at the policemen. "All right then. What can I help you with?"

"Mrs. Richey, did you have a babysitter here last night?" the shorter one asked as his partner took a notebook from his shirt pocket.

"Yes. Carly. Carly Neath. Why?"

They ignored her question and continued with their own. "Carly's mother says her daughter has worked for you before. Is that right?"

"Yes, Carly's been here several times this summer. My girls are crazy about her."

"What time was she here?"

"She came at seven o'clock and stayed until we got home around eleven. Actually, it was just about eleven-thirty." Helen absentmindedly fingered the fringe of the kitchen towel as the front door opened and her husband and daughters entered the tent. Jonathan stopped short when he saw the policemen but quickly introduced himself and shook hands with the officers.

"Why don't you girls go outside and water the flowers while Mommy and I talk to these nice policemen?" he suggested.

As soon as the girls were out of earshot, Helen explained what had been going on. "The police want to know about Carly. I was just telling them that we got home around eleven-thirty."

"So you got home about eleven-thirty," the officer taking the notes pondered out loud. "And then what happened?"

"I wanted to walk her home, but Carly insisted on going alone. We paid her, and she ran out the door before we could stop her," Jonathan answered.

Helen bit her lower lip and didn't contradict her husband. "Please, tell me. Has something happened to Carly?" she asked.

The officers rose from their chairs. "We hope not, ma'am. But her parents say Carly didn't come home last night. That's not necessarily something to get riled up about. Kids pull this kind of stunt all the time, and normally, we'd wait to see if she turned up later today or tomorrow. But with what happened earlier this week with the Patterson girl, we're getting involved right away."

"I thought Leslie Patterson faked her own abduction. That's what I heard anyway," Helen said.

"We can't comment on an ongoing investigation, ma'am."

"No, of course not. I understand that. But if something has happened to Carly—if she was kidnapped or something—maybe there really is some sort of lunatic out there."

The policeman didn't respond. But Jonathan put his arm around his wife's shoulder. "Don't worry, honey," he said.

As Helen watched the officers walk down the steps, she replayed the events of the night before in her mind. The babysitter had rushed out before Jonathan had gotten back from parking the car. In fact, it had been a good thirty minutes after Carly left before

Jonathan had returned to the tent. Helen had just assumed that her husband had had a hard time finding a parking spot. If she were honest with herself, she had been hoping it would take him as long as possible. Helen was determined to avoid doing her wifely duty. She didn't want to fight with him about it.

Helen dreaded marital intimacy in the close confines of the tent. The girls were sleeping so nearby, and the neighbors were able to hear the slightest noise. She'd pretended she was already asleep when she heard the screen door creak open, knowing that Jonathan would soon be nudging at her. But he hadn't. Her husband had undressed, slipped between the cotton sheets, and fallen asleep without even touching her.

Last night, she had been relieved. This morning the half hour that had led to her reprieve was time unaccounted for, time she wasn't sure where her husband had been. And just now, Jonathan had deliberately misled the police, indicating he had been here in the tent all along.

She waited until Sarah and Hannah were getting their bathing suits on and then beckoned to Jonathan to follow her to the kitchen.

"Why did you tell them that *you* wanted to walk Carly home? That *we* paid her? You weren't even here, Jonathan. Why did you lie?" Helen's clean, scrubbed face appeared solemn and worried as she whispered.

"Would it have been better for me to say I wasn't

here, Helen?" he countered. "I heard about Carly going missing in town just now. I don't want the cops looking at me as a suspect. Do *you?*"

CHAPTER 24

"Hi. It's Matthew. I'm in the lobby."

"Okay. I'll be right down."

Diane flipped her cell phone closed. Turning to her sister, she said, "I'm sorry, Em, but I have to get going. Please tell me again that you're all right with this."

Emily slid her emptied suitcase under her twin bed and stood up. "Will you stop worrying, Diane? We're going to be fine. The kids and I will find plenty to do. The first thing on the agenda is getting our suits on and hitting the beach."

"What would I do without you, Em?"

"Don't worry, you can pay me back when I have kids—if you aren't too old to handle it by then."

"Funny, Emily. Very funny."

Diane grabbed a bottle of sunscreen and threw her sunglasses and cell phone in her canvas tote bag. Pulling out her wallet, she counted off several twenty-dollar bills and handed them to Emily. After making hurried stops in Michelle's and Anthony's rooms to say good-bye, she rushed down the wooden staircase.

Matthew stood at the foot of the stairs, dressed in a

red KEY News T-shirt, khaki Bermuda shorts, and brown sandals.

"You lucky dog. I wish I could be wearing what you are."

"That's why it's great to work behind the camera." Matthew smiled as he gestured toward the door at the side of the lobby. "Want to go in there and sit down? We can get organized before we head out."

No one was in the old parlor, but a pitcher of iced tea and sparkling glasses were arranged on a gleaming silver tray on the refectory table at the side of the room. A basket packed with daisies sat on the mantel. They were nice touches in an otherwise tired space. Diane looked around, noticing the intricate molding along the edges of the high ceiling, the carved stone that framed the fireplace, the dulled bronze chandelier. The room had been neglected for years, but it had good bones. With some attention and good taste, it could be a Victorian showplace.

They poured themselves some iced tea and took seats on either end of the sofa. Matthew began to outline his game plan. "First and foremost, of course, we need to get Leslie Patterson. Our story cries for an interview with her."

Diane nodded. "That's my job. I'm going to call her mother again as soon as we finish here."

Matthew took a small spiral notebook from his knapsack and flipped back a few pages. "You could do that. But maybe it would be a better approach to go see her in person."

Diane wasn't enthusiastic about this suggestion. "You mean just go over to her house and knock on the door? I hate doing that."

"Actually, I was thinking that you could go to her store." He consulted his notes. "The mom runs a gift shop called Lavender & Lace. The Pattersons used it as a headquarters for the volunteers who searched for Leslie."

"I guess I could do that," Diane mused as she took a sip of tea. "But I'll go alone, without you or the crew. I don't want the poor woman to feel like she's being ambushed. Are you sure she'll even be there?"

"Well, she's supposed to be. I stopped over there when I got down here late yesterday afternoon, and a letter was taped to the front door. It thanked the community for their concern about Leslie and said that the store would reopen for business this weekend."

Diane jotted down the Main Avenue address in her own notebook. "What else?" she asked.

"The police have scheduled a noon press conference."

"About charges being pressed against Leslie?"

"I doubt it. That will probably come from the D.A.'s office. No, I'm not sure what the cops want to say. But I'll go over and cover it with the crew."

"That reminds me," said Diane. "What's with Sammy Gates using one of my rooms here?"

"Oh, God." Matthew groaned. "I'm sorry, Diane, but when Sammy saw his room in our motel, he threatened to go back to New York. I had to appease him. I just wish it wasn't at your expense."

Diane was skeptical. "You mean the place you're staying at is worse than this?"

Matthew uttered a low laugh. "The hole we're staying in makes the Dancing Dunes Inn look like a palace. These accommodations were the best I could do on such short notice. The shore places are booked months in advance."

"So, you and Gary Bing are stuck in a fleabag. I'm sorry, Matthew."

"Ah, it's no big deal. We won't be there much." Matthew glanced at his watch. "I better get going. I told Gates and Bing I'd meet them at the police station. Want me to drop you at Audrey Patterson's store?"

"Yeah, thanks. Let me get that over with."

CHAPTER 25

A bell tinkled as Diane opened the front door to Lavender & Lace. The shop's cool air was filled with the aromas of potpourri and scented candles. Embroidered linens, fine lace, and hand-milled soaps were displayed on white shelves that lined the lavender walls. Antique hat pins stood in tall porcelain holders, while boxes of ornate stationery and greeting cards crowded the counters. There were gaily colored parasols in umbrella stands, a display case full of fanciful gloves and feathered fans, and dozens of beaded evening bags hung from tiny hooks throughout the store. As she surveyed the room, Diane wondered how a search headquarters could possibly have existed in this place. There wasn't enough room for one more stickpin, let alone a small army of volunteers.

She paused to look at the collection of stuffed teddy bears that were arrayed on the steps of an old wooden ladder. Each was dressed in a lavender taffeta skirt, wore a matching wide-brimmed bonnet with lace trim, had a strand of faux pearls draped around its neck, and held a feathered fan in one of its paws.

A trim, middle-aged woman came out from behind the beaded curtain that covered a door at the back of the shop. She managed a wan smile as she navigated her way down the narrow aisle toward Diane.

"May I help you?" the woman asked automatically, pushing strands of gray-streaked hair behind her ear.

"These are delightful," said Diane, picking up one of the bears.

"Thank you. I've been carrying them for years, ever since my daughter fell in love with hers."

Diane put the bear back on the ladder step. "Are you Mrs. Patterson?"

"Yes." There was caution in the woman's voice.

Diane took off her sunglasses and extended her hand. "I'm Diane Mayfield."

"Oh." Audrey Patterson was flustered. "Forgive me.

I didn't recognize you. I'm so sorry. I guess I have too much on my mind."

"Please. There's absolutely nothing to apologize for. I shouldn't have left my sunglasses on."

Diane could feel Audrey studying her face. *She's looking for every line and wrinkle,* she thought—just like most people do when they meet someone they've seen only on television. She'll want to tell her friends that the KEY News personality looked prettier, homelier, thinner, fatter, older, younger in real life than she does on the screen.

"I was hoping that we might be able to talk some more," she said, getting to the point.

"About Leslie being on your show, right?"

"About interviewing her. Yes."

The bell at the front of the shop rang as a pair of older women walked inside.

"Let's go to the back," Audrey suggested.

"I can wait, if you need to help your customers," offered Diane.

"No, come on." Audrey lowered her voice to a whisper. "Those two are in here all the time. They're browsers, not buyers."

They went through the beaded curtain into a large storage room. Cardboard shipping cartons had been stacked high against the walls to make room for trestle tables that were littered with used paper coffee cups and empty donut boxes. A map of Ocean Grove and the surrounding towns was mounted on a giant easel. Grids had been drawn in red crayon across the map, organizing search areas.

"Would you like to sit down?" Audrey indicated a metal folding chair.

"Thank you."

Audrey leaned against the corner of the table. "I talked about it with my husband last night, and he says we have to wait until we hire a lawyer and see if he thinks it's all right for you to talk to Leslie."

"When do you think that will be, Mrs. Patterson?"

"Lou is making more phone calls today. But you know, Leslie hasn't been officially charged with anything yet."

"Let's hope she isn't," Diane said with sincerity. "It would be a terrible ordeal for a young woman to go through. I have a daughter of my own, and I can imagine how worried you must be."

Tears welled up in Audrey's dark eyes. "How old is your daughter?"

"Fourteen."

"Fourteen," Audrey repeated. "That was the year Leslie started to have problems."

Diane felt a pang of anxiety as she thought of Michelle. The idea of her own daughter following Leslie Patterson's path was beyond distressing. But the journalist in her recognized an opportunity. Audrey Patterson was opening up, and Diane had to encourage her to keep going.

"What kinds of problems?" she asked gently.

"Eating problems." Audrey cast her head downward, as if ashamed. "She got thinner and thinner. She was exercising more and more. At first, I didn't think too much of it. I'll always blame myself for that. By the time I realized anything was really wrong and got her to a doctor, he diagnosed her as having anorexia."

"Was he able to help her?" Diane felt herself rooting hard for an affirmative answer.

"God knows, he's tried." Audrey shook her head. "Owen Messinger is a saint as far as I'm concerned. He's treated Leslie for all these years, and he's been unfailingly patient with her when I . . ." Audrey's voice trailed off, and a tear rolled down her cheek.

"Why is it that mothers always blame themselves?" Diane asked gently. But the real question she wanted to ask was, If Owen Messinger was such a good therapist, eight years later why wasn't Leslie well?

CHAPTER 26

Matthew and the crew staked out their positions in front of the yellow concrete building on Central Avenue. Gary Bing attached a microphone to the wooden podium set up by the entry to the Ocean Grove substation of the Neptune Township Police Department. Sammy Gates picked out an advantageous spot to set up his camera.

Finding a tree to stand under as protection from the blazing sun, Matthew relaxed as he scanned the competition and waited for the news conference to begin.

There was no other national network news presence, though New Jersey Network was represented. So was WCBS. A couple of print reporters, notebooks poised, stood at the curb. All in all, less media representation than might have been expected. Yet Matthew wasn't all that surprised. Given ever-decreasing attention spans and limited coverage resources, assignment editors had chosen not to send any of the few camera crews they had on the weekends to follow up on the Leslie Patterson story . . . a story that could be considered old in a twenty-four-hour news cycle. Leslie Patterson went missing, Leslie Patterson had been found, and police thought Leslie Patterson had staged the whole thing. The television editors were making an educated guess: there wasn't going to be anything announced at this news conference that couldn't just as easily be told in twenty seconds by the anchor on the evening news. As long as an Associated Press reporter was there, the broadcast outlets were covered. They could get the information they needed from the wire service. The only reason KEY News had a crew here was that Joel Malcolm had a bee in his bonnet for this story for *Hourglass*.

The door of the station house opened. A police officer emerged and took his place at the podium.

"Can everyone hear me?" he asked. The broadcast technicians checked their meters.

"Go ahead," one of them yelled.

"I'm Chief Jared Albert of the Neptune Township Police Department."

"Spell it," the AP reporter shouted.

"J-A-R-E-D. A-L-B-E-R-T."

The officer paused before reading his prepared statement, waiting until the print reporters looked up from their notebooks.

"Early this morning, the Neptune Township Police Department was notifed by the parents of a twenty-year-old female Ocean Grove resident that their daughter had not returned home after a babysitting job last night. Because it comes on the heels of the disappearance of another Ocean Grove resident earlier this week, the Neptune Township Police Department is investigating this situation immediately and is appealing to the public and the press for help."

Matthew straightened from his slumped position beneath the shady branches of the tree and edged closer to the podium, where Chief Albert was holding up a photograph of a youthful, smiling face. The pretty blond wasn't Leslie Patterson. What was going on?

"This is Carly Rachel Neath. She is five feet, one inch tall and weighs approximately one hundred pounds. She is blond, blue-eyed, and has a birthmark on the inside of her left wrist. She was last seen wearing a pair of white hip-hugger slacks, a blue-and-white-striped halter-type shirt, and white leather sandals. Anyone with any information that might help in finding Carly Neath should notify the Neptune Township Police immediately."

Matthew snapped his gaze in the direction of

Sammy Gates. The cameraman had his video lens trained on the glossy picture. As Chief Albert finished his statement, Matthew shouted out the first questions. "What about Leslie Patterson? Does this mean that you no longer think she staged her own abduction, that the same person who kidnapped Leslie has now kidnapped Carly Neath? Are charges still going to be filed against Leslie?"

The police officer wiped the perspiration off his brow with the back of his hand before answering. "We are investigating all possibilities. At this time, no charges are being filed against Leslie Patterson."

CHAPTER 27

Carly opened her eyes but could see nothing. She realized that she was blindfolded. Her head throbbed so painfully that she was almost grateful for the darkness. Where was she?

The soft but persistent sound of dripping water felt closer than the roar of the ocean she could hear in the distance. Was that ruffling noise birds' wings above her? Was that cooing sound coming from a pigeon or a dove?

Shivering with fear, Carly lay on the damp ground and tried to recall what had happened. She'd been walking home, that was it. She'd left Shawn and was walking home from the Stone Pony. Now she remembered. She'd gotten mad at him and stalked out.

And then what? Carly concentrated despite the headache that made her pray for the relief of sleep. Gradually, the memory began to come back to her. She'd come out of the club and crossed the street. Then she'd had to decide which way she was taking back home. She'd chosen the shortcut around the old Casino when she was hit from behind and must have been knocked unconscious.

Was the pounding in her head from what hit her or was it one of her old migraines come back? Whatever its source, it was the worst pain she'd ever felt.

She had to get out of here. Carly struggled to get up, falling back again as she realized that her hands and feet were bound. The gag cut into the sides of her mouth as she tried to scream for help.

CHAPTER 28

After leaving Lavender & Lace, Diane found a bench beneath a tree on Main Avenue, sat down, and pulled out her cell phone to call information for the listing for Dr. Owen Messinger. Knowing that it was a long shot to reach him in his office on Saturday, she was about to try his number anyway when her phone rang. She glanced at the tiny identification screen before placing the device next to her ear.

"Hi, Matthew."

"Diane." There was urgency in his voice. "There's another girl missing."

"What?"

"Another young woman. Carly Neath. Just about the same age as Leslie Patterson. She never came home from her babysitting gig last night."

"And the police think there's a connection?" Diane asked.

"They didn't go so far as to say that, but they are pursuing it earlier than they would have at another time. And they say they aren't filing charges against Leslie."

"Wait till Joel hears. He'll be apoplectic," Diane predicted, thinking her boss could be agitated about this newest development. If another young woman was missing, was Leslie Patterson telling the truth? If Leslie hadn't cried wolf, would that leave her out as a subject for the *Hourglass* broadcast? But whether Joel decided to include Leslie Patterson or not, the fact that another young woman had been kidnapped was newsworthy on a national level. Matthew's next words didn't surprise Diane.

"*Weekend Evening Headlines* wants a piece on this tonight," he said.

"Let me guess. I'm the correspondent."

"Yes. The assignment desk doesn't have anyone in the Northeast Bureau to send down here. With the exception of the correspondent at the Broadcast Center who's there on bulletin duty, everyone is on vacation."

"Just like *we* should be," Diane said before switching into planning mode. "I'm starving. Let's get a little lunch and figure out where we're going. Oh, and Matthew? I haven't gotten the green light to interview Leslie Patterson yet. I don't know if Joel will even care anymore for *Hourglass*, but I'd love to get her reaction to Carly Neath's disappearance for the *Evening Headlines* piece."

Ten minutes later Diane and Matthew were escorted to a table in the open-air courtyard of the Starving Artist.

"You don't have a table inside by any chance, do you?" Matthew asked the host.

"Sorry. Everything inside is taken. Everybody wants the air-conditioning."

They ordered two iced teas right away and scanned the restaurant offerings.

"There are lots of things I love on this menu, but I'm too hot to eat them," Diane said. "I guess I'll go with the tuna salad platter."

"It's a double Italian-style hot dog and fries for me." Matthew closed the menu. "I'm never too hot to eat."

After placing their orders, he laid out what they had so far. "Okay, we've got the police presser and a picture of the second missing girl. We also have pictures of Leslie Patterson and the search for her earlier this week."

"Where did you get those?" Diane asked. "We weren't here."

"Well, I don't actually have them in my hands, but I

107

called the WKEY local desk, and they are going to dub off what they have and bring it over to the *Weekend Evening Headlines* studio. Since we didn't bring editing gear with us, we'll feed our material back to the Broadcast Center, and they'll edit the piece up there."

"When will the satellite truck get here?" Diane asked.

"About four o'clock. We'll want to feed at five."

She looked at her watch. "Okay, so we've got about four hours to see what other elements we can gather and then write the piece." She continued, "Of course, one of the best things we could get is still an interview with Leslie Patterson."

"Her mother wasn't biting, huh?"

"No. But that was before Carly Neath was declared missing. That changes the landscape considerably. Now it looks like Leslie Patterson could be telling the truth."

CHAPTER 29

Shawn walked into Nagle's and took his usual place at the counter. It was too late for breakfast, so he ordered a close approximation as his first food of the day.

"Egg salad on toasted rye and a cup of coffee," he instructed the thin, brown-haired waitress behind the counter. Shawn knew Anna because he and Carly had given her a ride to a doctor's appointment one night last week when Anna's old car was in the shop. She was staring at him now as if she had something she wanted to say. Shawn looked across the counter at her expectantly.

"Have you heard about Carly?"

"Heard what?" asked Shawn.

"Carly didn't come home last night. Her parents are frantic, and the police are out looking for her." Anna looked at him with some compassion. "She was supposed to come home after her babysitting job, but she didn't. No one knows where she is. I'm going to have to do a double shift to cover for her."

Shawn slid off the counter stool. "Cancel my order, will you, Anna?"

He escaped outdoors but didn't feel the scorching rays of the sun or the hot, still air. Shawn's mind raced. He should go talk to the police before the police came to talk to him. It was just a matter of time before they found out that he had been with Carly last night at the Stone Pony. If the Nagle's waitress recognized him as Carly's boyfriend, there were others who would as well.

If he told the police the truth, it was going to look bad. He had fought with Carly, just as he had fought with Leslie right before she disappeared. He was the obvious common denominator between the two women.

Shawn knew from the questioning he'd gone through when Leslie disappeared that the police had looked at him as a prime suspect. He knew from the course he'd taken on family violence that women were most often attacked not by strangers but by people they knew—disgruntled boyfriends or husbands leading the pack.

Closing his eyes and running his nail-bitten fingers back through his hair in desperation, Shawn knew that he had to think of something. The police were going to think he was responsible for Carly's disappearance, and they'd go back and try to pin Leslie's on him, too.

CHAPTER 30

"Do you believe me now?"

Audrey jumped as her daughter spoke from behind her.

"Don't sneak up on me like that, Leslie. You scared me to death." She turned around but continued sorting through a box of scented candles. "I didn't hear the bell at the front door ring when you came in. I guess my mind is on other things."

Seeing the look of resignation on her mother's face, Leslie asked, "You haven't heard yet, have you?"

"What?"

"There's another girl missing." Leslie's brown eyes were bright with excitement.

Audrey put the box of candles on the counter and leaned against the edge.

"Mom? Did you hear me? There's another girl missing. The police will believe me now. Everyone will believe me."

"Leslie!" Audrey hissed. "Lower your voice, will you please?"

Leslie's thin face darkened. "Well, I thought you might be happy for me, Mom. Don't you see? This proves I was telling the truth."

"Of course I'm relieved that you will be vindicated, dear." Audrey reached out to stroke her daughter's fine brown hair, noticing it had lost some of its sheen. "But, honestly, it's hard to be happy at some other poor girl's expense. Who is she? Do I know her?"

"I doubt it. But she's a waitress at Nagle's, and she's the one Shawn's been going out with."

"Dear God," Audrey exclaimed. "Another girlfriend of Shawn's disappeared? The police *must* be looking into that. Well, God help her, and God help her family," Audrey said softly, thinking about what she and her husband had just been through. "I think we should do something to help them, Leslie. Maybe we should volunteer our storeroom again as a community search headquarters."

Audrey could almost see the wheels spinning in her daughter's mind before she answered. "Yeah, I guess that would be okay. And I'll come in to help. I want everyone who doubted me to have a chance to tell me how wrong they were."

CHAPTER 31

Trudging up Main Avenue, Sammy Gates grumbled as he carried his heavy camera gear over his shoulder. "Jesus, it's hot. Remind me again why we're doing this."

"Because if we can't get Leslie Patterson, at least we might get some reaction from her mother." Diane tried to sound patient, but inwardly she was in no mood for Sammy's complaints. This was his job, for God's sake. "If she agrees, and we're ready to shoot right then, she won't have time to change her mind."

"Sounds half-baked to me." Sammy sneered as he turned to his partner. "What do you think, Gary?"

"It makes no difference." Gary shrugged. "I'm on the clock, and whatever they want while they're paying the freight is fine by me." Gary Bing was as sweet and agreeable as Sammy Gates was ornery and argumentative. Diane thought Gary was a saint for working with Sammy. While most KEY News staffers avoided Sammy as much as possible, poor Gary was stuck with the curmudgeon day after day.

Sammy didn't take the cue his partner offered. Instead, he continued with his litany of complaints. "And the accommodations here leave a lot to be desired. I like a television set in my room, and I'm not into hooked rugs and sharing a bathroom at the end of the hall."

"Matthew told me the Dancing Dunes Inn is much nicer than the place you were originally going to stay in," said Diane, still a bit resentful that her family had been forced to give up one of their rooms to make Sammy happy. "It's tired, but it's clean and really charming in places."

"Charming, schmarming. It's a dump too. Give me a Marriott any day. Room service and a minibar, that's for me."

Diane held her hand up, cutting Sammy's complaints short. "Look. I think that's Leslie Patterson."

Across the street, a very thin figure was stepping from the curb in front of Lavender & Lace. "Get ready, you guys," she ordered as she scooted between cars cruising on the main street. "Leslie? Leslie Patterson?" she called to the young female, who backed up again onto the sidewalk.

As Diane got closer, she took a deep breath. Though she knew that Leslie was eight years older than her own daughter, the young woman didn't look it. It was almost as if she was stuck in adolescence. The legs that poked out from her denim shorts had none of the feminine curves associated with a little meat on one's bones, and she had hardly any chest at all.

"I know who you are," Leslie said proudly. "You're Diane Mayfield from KEY News."

Diane held out her hand. "Nice to meet you, Leslie."

"My mother told me you called yesterday about interviewing me."

"That's right," Diane said. "And I can certainly

understand why she didn't agree to it yesterday, or even this morning when I went to see her. But now, with the other girl's disappearance, I was hoping you and your mother might reconsider."

"I don't need my mother's permission, Diane," Leslie said. "I'm an adult."

"That's true enough," agreed Diane. "But under the circumstances, it might be best to consult her." She knew it was the mother in her offering the counsel. She hoped if, God forbid, Michelle were ever in a situation like Leslie's, her daughter would turn to her for maternal advice.

"I don't have to talk to my mother about it," Leslie said as she looked over Diane's shoulder and eyed the camera crew.

What was she going to do? Insist that Leslie get her mother's approval? Leslie was legally an adult. If the young woman agreed to the interview, Diane would be a fool not to ask the questions.

"All right," she said, turning to Gary. "Mike her up, will you? We can do it right here on the sidewalk."

Leslie was one step ahead of her and, Diane realized at that moment, extremely media savvy. "Why don't we go over to the Beersheba Well, where the security guard found me? It's just a couple of blocks from here. We could do the interview there."

Sammy set up his tripod. Gary clipped a little microphone to the collar of Leslie's sleeveless blouse and handed her a small black battery pack. "Here. Slide the wire from the mike under your shirt, and clip the power pack to the back of your shorts."

Leslie obeyed. "Don't I get a makeup woman or something?"

Diane smiled. "Sorry. If we were in the studio in New York, yes. But out here in the field, it's every woman for herself." She pulled out a makeup case and hand mirror from her bag. "Would you like a little blush?"

Leslie nodded.

Diane selected the most youthful colors from the collection of cosmetics she kept with her virtually all the time. A peachy lipstick and blush and a dark brown mascara would work best with Leslie's coloring.

While reapplying her own lipstick, powdering her face, brushing her hair, and hitting it with some hair spray, Diane made small talk, asking Leslie what she was planning to do now that she was free again.

"I'm going back to work on Monday, but this whole thing has made me realize I want to do more with my life. I hope I can go a bit further than the office job I have at Surfside Realty."

"What are your duties now?" Diane asked politely.

"You know . . . answering phones and sending faxes, going through the mail, ordering things for the office."

Diane saw the crew had finished setting up. "Leslie, why don't you and I stand over here beside the gazebo?" she suggested.

Leslie tentatively took her place beside Diane. "It's strange being back here now, when it was just two nights ago that they found me here."

Diane reached out to pat Leslie's arm. "Don't worry. It's going to be all right." She turned to the crew. "All set, you guys?"

"Go," Sammy ordered.

"All set, Leslie?" Diane asked.

"Uh-huh."

Diane turned to her and began. "We're here, sitting together on the spot where you were found very early Friday morning after having been missing for three days. Tell me what happened to you, Leslie."

Leslie sighed heavily before answering. "I was walking on the boardwalk late Monday night when someone came up behind me and knocked me out. When I came to, I was blindfolded and bound, and there was some sort of rag tied around my mouth so I couldn't call for help. I didn't know where I was." She rubbed her bare arms, as if trying to get warm.

"That must have been terrifying."

Leslie nodded but said nothing.

"What happened then?" Diane urged.

"Well, he—I'm guessing it was 'he' because who-ever it was never spoke to me—he just left me lying there, wherever 'there' was. He would come back once in a while to bring me something to eat, but I ate very little. And each time he came back, he would pull me up and want me to dance with him."

"Dance with him? I don't understand," said Diane.

"There was no music or anything, but I think you'd call it dancing. He'd pull me up and press his body

116

against me, rocking back and forth, almost in rhythm with the waves flowing in. We must have been near the ocean. I could hear it."

With every word Leslie spoke, Diane was more certain that the piece she would be offering on *Weekend Evening Headlines* in a few hours would be mesmerizing.

"It was horrible. So horrible. The only way I could get through it was thinking of dancing with my boyfriend Shawn." Leslie's voice rose plaintively. "But the worst part is that I don't think anyone believed me."

"Another young woman is missing, Leslie. Do you think people will believe you now?"

"I hope so," Leslie answered softly as tears welled up in her brown eyes. "And I feel sorry for her."

CHAPTER 32

Though Carly Neath's father said neither he nor his wife would have anything to say to the press, Matthew thought it was a good idea to go over to their house anyway. People could easily say no on the phone, but when actually face-to-face with another human being, they sometimes changed their minds. Without the intimidation of a camera crew, Matthew felt he might have a better chance of getting the Neaths to talk with him.

He found the house in the middle of the block on Surf Avenue. There were no shutters or window boxes on the aluminum-sided colonial. Though it was a bland dwelling now, Matthew suspected that beneath the worn white siding there were the wooden boards and elaborate moldings of the original Victorian structure. Someone's idea of progress had left the house totally without charm.

He knocked on the front door, waited, and then knocked again. Matthew couldn't be sure if the Neaths were inside or not. He pressed his cupped hands against the window and tried to see through the glass.

"They're in there all right."

Matthew spun around in the direction of the voice. A very elderly man stood on the porch of the house next door.

"I know they're in there in case that daughter of theirs calls. They don't want to miss out if the police call with news, neither."

Matthew walked away from Neaths' front door, sensing that this old guy, with his bony shoulders and arms sticking out of his sleeveless undershirt, might be a good source of information. He went next door and struck up a conversation.

"So, I guess you know Carly?"

"Yep. I've known her since she was a little kid. Always gettin' into everything, that one. It looks like she got into something bad this time."

"Have any theories on what might have happened to her?" Matthew asked.

The old man shrugged his shoulders. "I have my suspicions."

Matthew waited for the man to continue.

"You know, it's tough gettin' old. You don't even think about that now, do you, sonny?"

"Not much," Matthew said, noticing the flaking skin at the man's temples. There were a couple of teeth missing from the old guy's bottom gums, and a vague odor of decay reached Matthew's nostrils.

"I didn't think about it when I was your age either. But it comes before you know it. And it brings with it all sorts of miserable things. For me, the worst is not sleepin'. Can't tell you when the last time I slept through the night was."

"That's too bad," said Matthew, wishing the old codger would get to the point. The man took a seat in the rocking chair on his porch.

"It was so hot last night. Lord, was it hot. I don't have air-conditionin'. Don't usually need it here, even in the summertime. And it costs money to run those things, and that's something I don't have enough of."

Matthew was growing impatient. He had to keep himself from tapping his foot on the porch floor. Instead, he nodded in agreement, as if he understood the old man's problems.

"So I came out here to sit in my rocker because I thought it would be cooler. But it wasn't. I expect it was just about as hot as inside."

Matthew anticipated where this was going and

wanted to move things along. "So you saw something from here on your porch last night?"

The man rocked. "Yep."

"What did you see?" The old guy seemed to be enjoying stringing this out.

"I could see Carly walkin' up the street. That yellow hair of hers was catchin' the moonlight."

"What time was that?" Matthew asked.

"About eleven-thirty, quarter to twelve."

"Did you say anything to her, or did she say anything to you?"

"She didn't even see me, and I didn't have nothin' to say to her."

The elderly man paused, enjoying his power. After rocking for a minute, he continued. "Well, I might as well tell you what I told the police when they were here today askin' all their questions. I wasn't a bit surprised when I saw it. You know these kids today, comin' and goin' at all hours of the day and night. Even the girls. In my day, no self-respectin' girl would be out by herself alone at night like that. Even here in Ocean Grove."

"What did you see?" Matthew pressed him.

"I seen her walk right by her own house and keep on goin'." The old man shook his head. "Yep. She just kept on walkin'. Toward the ocean. Late at night like that. It's a disgrace what young girls do today."

"So, you said you had your suspicions about what happened to Carly." Matthew tried diverting the man's attention from the mores of today's youth.

"What do you think happened?" He leaned forward to hear.

"Like I told the police. I think that guy got her."

"Guy? What guy?"

"The one that was following along behind her. She didn't see him, but he sure was makin' a beeline for her."

CHAPTER 33

A small, curious crowd gathered on the grass surrounding the red gazebo that covered the Beersheba Well to watch the news team shooting the interview. Diane was used to the gawks and stares, but Leslie was not. It wasn't that she didn't enjoy attention, but Leslie was uncomfortable about exposing herself in front of people she didn't know. Somehow, anonymous television viewers didn't unnerve her nearly as much as the real human beings straining to hear what she was telling Diane Mayfield.

"I think that's all I have to say right now." Leslie pulled at her microphone.

Diane knew better than to push. She would want another opportunity to interview Leslie at greater length for the *Hourglass* segment if Joel decided to go ahead with it. For now, she had more than enough for the relatively short piece for *Evening Headlines*. And, on a more personal level, Diane didn't want to force anyone else's daughter to do something against her will.

"What time will this be on?" Leslie asked as she stood up.

"I'm not sure where the story will be scheduled in the show, but the broadcast begins at six-thirty," Diane answered. "Thank you so much for doing this, Leslie. We really appreciate it."

Diane watched the young woman make her way through the onlookers, cut across the lawn, and head back toward the heart of town. As Sammy and Gary packed up their gear, Diane sat back down on the well's step and took a notebook from her bag. She was beginning to rough out a script when her cell phone rang.

"This call is from a federal prison," announced the recorded voice.

Diane knew the drill. When prompted, she pressed five to accept the call.

"It's me."

In spite of everything, his voice never failed to thrill her. Since the first time he had spoken to her, back in that psychology class in senior year in college, she'd been a sucker for his soft West Virginia drawl. Diane got up, turned her back, and walked away from the camera crew.

"Hi, it's me," she answered softly.

"Well? How is it? How was the flight? Have you hooked up with the tour yet?" His questions were rapid-fire.

Diane bit the inside of her mouth.

"Diane? Are you there?"

"Yes, Philip. I'm here."

"Well? How's it going? Are the kids all excited? Tell me what's going on." There was such enthusiasm in his voice, Diane hated to disappoint him. She knew he was craving some happy news; he needed to have something to think about after lights out, when sleep would not come.

"Actually, Philip, there's been a change in plans."

"This call is from a federal prison." The recorded voice again, interrupting and reminding them of something they never forgot.

"What kind of change of plans?" There was wariness in Philip's voice. "Has something happened? Is something wrong? Are the kids sick?" Now there was panic in his tone.

"No, Michelle and Anthony are fine," she quickly reassured him. There was no way Diane was going to discuss her fears about Michelle and a possible eating disorder now. Philip couldn't do a thing about it, and there was no point in giving him more to worry about.

"Are you okay, honey?" he asked.

At the term of endearment, Diane felt a tug in her chest. For richer, for poorer, in sickness and in health . . . Despite her disappointment at what he had done professionally and her anger at what his actions had done to their family, Diane still hoped that, with time, she would be able to forgive her husband. What they'd had together once had been so good. Even though

Philip had made a terrible mistake, she hadn't stopped—couldn't stop—loving him. They had too much history. They shared two children. And their emotional and physical chemistry had always been strong.

How she ached to be with Philip again. Not in some large room with theater-style seating, with prison guards and security cameras watching. Knowing that, when the visit ended, he would be forced to go through the indignity of a strip search. Dear God, she wanted their old life back, with all the privacy they had taken so much for granted.

"I'm fine, Philip. Really. But I had to cancel the vacation. Joel Malcolm insisted I cover a story."

"Ah, Di, you're kidding." The disappointment in his voice was palpable.

"I wish I were, believe me, but I'm not. Instead I'm in Ocean Grove, New Jersey, doing a story on missing girls."

"And where are the kids? They must have been so bummed out."

"That's an understatement, especially Anthony. But Joel said I could bring them with me. They're probably with Emily at the beach right now."

"This call is from a federal prison." Again, the damned recording.

"I have to get back to my room for the four o'clock count, Di." His voice sounded heavy.

The thought of Philip standing up and being counted as a criminal by prison officers sickened her. In fact, everything she knew about what Philip was forced to endure at the federal prison sickened her. What she didn't know, the things she suspected he didn't tell her, truly terrified her.

But he had committed a crime, and if there was any chance he or they could go forward and live an honest life, Philip had to pay for what he had done.

CHAPTER 34

The KEY News satellite truck operator parked his rig at the designated meeting place, the cul-de-sac at the end of Ocean Avenue. Leaving the motor running, Scott Huffman sat back to wait for Diane Mayfield and Matthew Voigt and whichever their crew was for this *Weekend Evening Headlines* assignment. The view out the window was a reminder that it was a summer weekend and he was working yet again. People in shorts and bathing suits strolled on the boardwalk. Some were filing into a large wood-frame structure that backed up to the beach. Others were lined up in front at a take-out window.

Scott's stomach rumbled, recalling that it hadn't been fed anything since the cheese Danish and coffee early in the morning. When he opened the door of the truck, the hot blast of air that pushed inside tempted him to stay put in the nice, cool cab. But hunger trumped comfort. He got out of the van, locked it up, and joined the others waiting in line.

Scott paid for two hot dogs with the works, fries, and a root beer. He didn't want to stink up the truck, so he carried the cardboard tray with his order to a bench farther down the boardwalk. He wolfed down the late lunch, gazing out at the ocean between bites.

As he chewed, he thought about himself. He had to get a life. Sure, the overtime was great, but he hadn't spent a full weekend at home the whole summer. Last month he'd been away for over a week when *KEY to America* had broadcast from Newport, Rhode Island. It wasn't fair to his wife and kids, and it wasn't fair to himself. He didn't want to become one of those guys who missed the important things just to have a bigger cushion in the bank. He had to start saying no to the weekend assignments. There were other guys who could run the satellite rig and feed the audio and video back to the Broadcast Center. Let *them* get the over-time.

Scott tossed the trash from his lunch into a garbage can and headed back up the boardwalk, passing a guy who might have been about his own age going in the other direction. Despite the oppressive heat, the man was wearing pants and a long-sleeved military cam-ouflage shirt. He was muttering to himself. Scott couldn't help staring at the guy. It was clear something wasn't quite right with him.

There's a troubled soul who really got screwed in the lottery of life, he thought. But as he spotted Diane Mayfield waving beside the satellite truck, the pathetic stranger was quickly forgotten.

126

CHAPTER 35

Diane was in the satellite truck, putting the finishing touches on her script, when her cell phone sounded. She listened as Matthew filled her in on what Carly Neath's neighbor said he had seen the night before.

"Wow," said Diane. "Think we should add something about Carly's being followed to the script?"

"I'd feel better about it if we had the police comment on it," Matthew replied, "but nobody is returning my calls."

"I wish you'd had the crew with you, Matthew. Think your witness would say it all again for the camera? If we had him on tape saying that he saw someone following Carly, the piece would be stronger."

"It's worth a shot. Send Sammy and Gary over, and I'll see if I can get the old guy to say it again."

"And guess what?" Diane asked after jotting down the address. "Leslie Patterson talked to us."

"You're kidding. That's great! Good stuff?"

"Enough. I think we're in good shape for tonight's story. But I'll want to get her later for the *Hourglass* segment. Once we see what happens with Carly Neath, we'll need more reaction from Leslie."

After instructing the camera crew to go to Surf Avenue, Diane looked at her script again and made the adjustments necessary to include a sound bite from

Carly's neighbor. She also wrote an alternate line of track, explaining what the witness had seen, in case Matthew was unsuccessful in securing another interview. The extra narration could be edited in at the last minute if necessary.

Satisfied it was set to be read by the executive producer at the Broadcast Center, Diane clicked the SEND icon on the computer and sat back to wait for script approval.

CHAPTER 36

It wasn't long into the police questioning that Shawn realized he should have brought an attorney with him. So he waited for another two hours until the public defender arrived at the station house. The guy was dressed in a golf shirt and Bermuda shorts, as if he'd been called away from a round of golf or a family barbecue. After getting up to speed on Shawn's version of what had happened so far, the lawyer signaled that the officers could come back into the small interrogation area.

"My client came in here of his own free will," the attorney began. "He's told you that he was with Carly Neath last night, that she walked out on him at the Stone Pony, and that that was the last he saw of her. Unless you have something to book him on, we're outta here."

"So it's just a coincidence that the young woman who was abducted earlier this week happened to be a girlfriend of his as well?" one detective asked.

"That's sure the way it looks," the lawyer said, keeping his face expressionless.

The other detective shook his head, knowing that, for now anyway, their hands were tied. They needed to get some solid evidence on the guy. "All right, Ostrander," he snarled. "Get out of here. But don't go anywhere we can't reach you."

CHAPTER 37

"The old guy won't talk again, Diane. We're not going to have his sound bite for the piece."

"All right. We'll go with Plan B. Thanks, Matthew."

Diane flipped the phone closed and picked up the lip mike. Holding it close to her mouth, she began recording the approved track.

"For the second time in less than a week, a young woman has gone missing in an idyllic New Jersey shore town. Twenty-year-old Carly Neath did not return home last night after finishing her babysitting job in the quiet, picturesque town of Ocean Grove."

She paused to give the instructions on inserting a sound bite from the police news conference. "Use the bite we'll feed you after the track. It's Chief Jared Albert, J-A-R-E-D A-L-B-E-R-T, Neptune Township

Police Department. The sound bite is: 'Coming on the heels of the disappearance of another Ocean Grove resident earlier this week, the Neptune Township Police Department is investigating this situation immediately and is appealing to the public and the press for help.'"

Diane cleared her throat. "Track two: Police and volunteers are scouring the town known as 'God's Little Acre,' a square-mile community an hour from New York City, as they did just days ago for twenty-two-year-old Leslie Patterson. After a three-day search, she was found, bound and gagged, on the grounds of the Ocean Grove Camp Meeting Association. There was speculation that Leslie might have staged her own abduction to get attention. But this latest disappearance changes things. Leslie spoke exclusively to KEY News today at the site where she was discovered early Friday morning."

Diane stopped to consult her notes on Leslie's interview. "Okay. The sound bite is: 'I was walking on the boardwalk late Monday night when someone came up behind me and knocked me out. When I came to, I was blindfolded and bound, and there was some sort of rag tied around my mouth so I couldn't call for help. I didn't know where I was.'"

Going back to the script, Diane continued. "Track three. Tonight, the search goes on for Carly Neath.

"Sound bite, Chief Albert again. 'She is five feet, one inch tall and weighs approximately one hundred pounds. She is blond, blue-eyed, and has a birthmark

130

on the inside of her left wrist. She was last seen wearing a pair of white hip-hugger slacks, a blue-and-white-striped halter-type shirt, and white leather sandals. Anyone with any information that might help in finding Carly Neath should notify the Neptune Township Police immediately.' "

Here was the spot she would have liked to include a sound bite from Carly's neighbor. Instead, Diane recorded the alternate lines she had written. "KEY News has learned that a witness has come forward with information that may provide a clue. A man was seen following Carly last night as she walked near her home. Whether that man had anything to do with Carly Neath's disappearance is unclear. But Leslie Patterson says she feels sorry for Carly and what she might be facing.

"Okay, pick up Leslie's sound bite in the middle of her sentence. Start with: 'whoever it was never spoke to me,' and then just continue on. 'Left me lying there, wherever "there" was. He would come back once in a while to bring me something to eat, but I ate very little. And each time he came back, he would pull me up and want me to dance with him.'

"Last track. Dancing a sick dance that family and friends pray Carly Neath is not performing now. Diane Mayfield, KEY News, Ocean Grove, New Jersey."

CHAPTER 38

The minute he walked through the door, Larry loosened his tie and kicked off his shoes. It had been a long day, but it had been worth it. Today was no different from every other Saturday this summer. He'd made a sale. Knock wood. Larry knew from painful experience that it was never truly a sale until the closing. When all the documents were signed and all the money had changed hands, then, and only then, did the real estate agent get paid his commission.

But Larry had a hunch this deal was money in the bank. The buyers were prequalified for their mortgage, and they had already lost two other houses in the heated market. They weren't going to make waves about anything that came up in the physical inspection of the property. They just wanted to secure their own place at the shore.

Larry popped open a beer, shuffled across the living room to switch on the television set, and settled back on the couch. He wished he had someone who would talk about his day and celebrate his success. This was when he missed his wife and daughter most. Going off to work in the morning from an empty house was bad enough, but coming home at night to face another dinner by himself was worse. Sitting alone, evening after evening, watching the boob tube, gave him too much time to think.

Propping his feet up on the coffee table, he aimed the remote control at the set and clicked. Golf was just wrapping up on KEY, and the network news was about to begin.

The first story was about the war in Iraq, the second about the president's day. Larry got up and went to the refrigerator again. As he uncapped another beer, he heard the words "Ocean Grove" and hurried back to the living room.

He watched the piece with its pretty pictures of Ocean Grove and a smiling Carly Neath, and listened to Diane Mayfield's narration. But he was especially interested in what Leslie had to say.

"He would come back once in a while to bring me something to eat, but I ate very little."

For Larry, those words, and the sight of Leslie's sharp jawline and thin arms, brought back the pain that never went away. The memories of Jenna and all the times he'd tried so unsuccessfully to get her to nourish herself. Larry had spent countless hours trying to think of and procure any morsel that might tempt his daughter. But nothing had worked. Jenna went from thin to skinny to gaunt to emaciated.

Leslie was his chance to make up, in some way, for his mistakes with his own daughter. He had to help Leslie, make her see that while her eating disorder was extremely serious, it was solvable, and the solution lay within her. Not with that quack therapist. Owen Messinger had ruined Jenna, and now he was having his way with Leslie as well.

Burping as he switched off the set, Larry wondered why Leslie couldn't see what she was doing to herself. She had to learn that there were much bigger problems out there, problems that people could truly do nothing about. Being held against one's will was certainly a good example. If that didn't scare a kid straight, what would?

Larry held out the hope that Leslie had learned something from her terrifying experience and that it would lead to a real change in her self-destructive behavior and outlook on life. He was looking forward to Monday. Leslie would be back at work, and he could keep an eye on her again.

CHAPTER 39

Owen Messinger stared at the television set long after the KEY *Weekend Evening Headlines* concluded. He had been stunned to see Leslie Patterson speaking in the report. Her mother had told him only yesterday that Leslie didn't want to go out of the house.

But with Carly Neath's disappearance, Owen supposed Leslie felt vindicated and wanted to say so. Perhaps all this ugliness would end up being a good thing for Leslie. It might, in some bizarre way, make her feel better about herself. If the community saw that they had misjudged her and that she had been telling the truth, sympathy would flow her way and Leslie would get positive attention. She could use that.

God knew, he wasn't getting anywhere with her. All these years and Leslie was still anguished about food and still cutting herself. His therapy wasn't working at all with her on the cutting score. He was worried about that.

Owen went to the bar in his dining room and poured himself a double Scotch. He studied the amber liquid in the glass, unsure what he should do next. He had been working on his innovative approach to treatment with enough success that he was almost ready to publish. But Leslie was the fly in the ointment. His results with her negatively skewed the predicted outcomes of his study.

"Here, Cleo," he called out. "Where are you, baby?" Owen walked over to his desk while he waited to see if the cat would appear. He sat down, determined to do something about the stack of mail that had been accumulating all week. First he sorted out all the catalogs and tossed them in the wastepaper basket. That act alone made him feel he'd made a nice dent. Next he separated out the bills. That left a couple magazines and just one envelope.

The black-and-white feline jumped into Owen's lap as he took the letter opener and sliced open the envelope. He stroked the cat's fur as he read the message inside.

YOU ARE A CHARLATAN.

THAT THERAPY OF YOURS HAS HAD TOO MANY VICTIMS.

IF THE POLICE OR THE MEDICAL COMMUNITY WERE TO FIND OUT WHAT YOU DO TO THESE POOR WOMEN, YOU WOULD LOSE YOUR LICENSE. BUT, IF YOU DECIDE TO GO TO THE AUTHORITIES, HERE'S MY CARD. I CAN'T WAIT TO TELL THE POLICE ALL ABOUT YOU.

OR, IF YOU WANT A PIECE OF ME, I'D BE GLAD TO TAKE YOU ON DIRECTLY. COME ON OVER.

LET THIS BE A WARNING TO YOU. CEASE AND DESIST BEFORE YOU DESTROY ANOTHER LIFE.

Owen picked up the white business card that had fluttered to the carpet. It read "Surfside Realty" and had Larry Belcaro's name emblazoned on it.

CHAPTER 40

When Diane got back to the Dancing Dunes, she found Anthony and Emily playing Scrabble in the parlor.

"I can see what you guys did today." She laughed. Both her son's and her sister's faces reflected the time spent out in the sun. "Does it hurt?"

"Quit worrying, Mom, will ya? We put on sunscreen."

"Where's Michelle?" Diane asked as she looked around the room and through the entry to the dining room.

"She's upstairs." Emily didn't take her eyes off the Scrabble board. "Queen. Q-U-E-E-N, and the Q is a triple-letter score," she said triumphantly.

Anthony's face fell, acknowledging the gap between himself and his aunt was almost insurmountable now. "I'm starving," he said. "When are we going to eat?"

"What are you in the mood for?" Diane asked, although the last thing in the world she wanted to do after the long, hot day she'd had was go out to dinner. A nice cool bath and long stretch on the bed in her air-conditioned room sounded infinitely more appealing. But this was their first night here, and she knew the kids and Em had been waiting for her.

"Pizza?" Anthony suggested.

"Em?"

"Fine with me."

"Great," said Diane, grateful that they wouldn't have to sit through a two-hour dinner service some-where. "Anthony, run up and get your sister, will you?"

While she waited for her children to come downstairs, Diane pulled out her cell phone and finally left the message at Dr. Owen Messinger's office that she would like to interview him about women's health issues for the *Hourglass* piece.

"Please call me at your earliest convenience," she said into the mouthpiece. "Of course, I understand you can't speak specifically about Leslie Patterson, but I do have some general questions our viewers would be interested in."

When asked for his suggestion, Carlos said they should drive over to Asbury Park to his favorite pizza parlor. "It's not long on atmosphere, but the pies are the best I've ever had."

Fifteen minutes later they were seated in the store-front restaurant. They ordered two pies, one just tomato and cheese, the other topped with pepperoni. Anthony dug right in, polishing off four slices in rapid succession. Emily and Diane both berated themselves for going for thirds. But Michelle took only one, nibbling at it and leaving all of the crust on her plate.

Diane hated the fact that she was keeping track now, watching every morsel of food that went into her daughter's mouth.

CHAPTER 41

Now that it was dark, it was as safe as it was ever going to be. The moonlight made going to the Casino risky, but there was nothing that could change that. It had to be done tonight.

Keeping close to the gently rounded outer wall of the Casino lessened the chance of being spotted. Around the curve, a breeze finally came in from the ocean, blowing at the giant copper sea horse that hung by metal threads, ready to snap from the roof of the neglected art deco building. A rickety fence blocked the entrance. Iridescent letters spelled DANGER: KEEP OUT. PRIVATE PROPERTY. NO TRESPASSING.

There was no difficulty slipping through the opening in the fence. Once inside, it was safe to turn on the flashlight. The yellow beam shot out over a wet cement floor strewn with bird droppings, broken shells, and seagull feathers. Bits of broken glass crunched underfoot.

Beneath the old sign that proclaimed the cavernous auditorium as the Casino Skating Palace, there was a hole in the wall, smaller than the one in the fence outside. It hadn't been easy dragging the dead weight of Carly's body through the hole last night, but traveling alone now, it was a snap to get in. There were more animal droppings and water damage on the wooden planks strewn around the neglected floor. Dominating the room was an abandoned stage, where in Asbury Park's heyday, so many popular acts had performed. It was now overgrown with brambles and littered with tar sheeting. Moss covered the long benches where fans once sat and cheered the summertime entertainment.

Rusted metal wagon-wheel-style chandeliers hung from the iron rafters. A thin shaft of light sifted through a hole in the roof. Strange. It almost seemed to point the way to the old refreshment counter, the place that was now Carly's hellhole.

It was essential that everything be done just so. Carly must go through the routine. It had been almost twenty-four hours since she'd been abducted and imprisoned. Now it was time to cut the plastic flex cuffs that bound Carly's ankles. It was time for her first dance.

CHAPTER 42

Carly couldn't see a thing, but she could hear just fine. Too well. She listened as the creature approached, shuffling through the debris. As the sounds grew closer, Carly couldn't tell if they were made by an animal or a man. She wasn't sure which would be worse.

She could feel her heart beating through her chest wall, reacting to the adrenaline shooting through her body. Her head was still throbbing, her wrists were sore and raw from whatever bound them. She tried to concentrate on her breathing, only able to take air in through her nose because the gag covered her mouth.

The footsteps stopped right beside her. A sliver of brightness slipped in through the thin opening at the bottom of Carly's blindfold. It must be a human being, who'd turned on the lights.

Carly felt tugging at her ankles and could feel the bonds slip off. Then her arm was gently grabbed and pulled upward. Maybe he was going to let her go.

She worked at getting to her feet, feeling dizzy and struggling to maintain her balance. Unable to make a sound, and not knowing what else to do, Carly stood and waited for what was coming next.

Hope was replaced with terror as the caressing began.

She wasn't sure how long it went on. A minute? Ten? Half an hour? It seemed like an eternity. Something smooth brushed back and forth across her cheeks and up and down her bare arms. Was it leather? A gloved hand?

And then a body pressed itself against hers and nudged her to move. Carly's hands were still bound, but she felt the fabric-covered arms wrap around her bare ones. She could hear soft swishing. Was that the sound of nylon rubbing against nylon? The sound ski pants made when they rubbed together as you walked through the snow?

As her tormentor's body started to rock to the rhythm of the tide, pulsing in and pulsing out, Carly's body automatically followed the lead. But she let her mind go to another place, trying to recall what it had been like to go sledding and make snowmen.

SUNDAY
AUGUST 21

CHAPTER 43

She opened her eyes and reached out for her watch on the table next to the bed. Diane was stunned to see it was almost ten o'clock and to realize that she'd slept soundly through the night.

She and Matthew had agreed that he would check with the police in the morning and then call her around noon to make their plans for the day. If there was anything to shoot earlier than that, Matthew and the crew would cover it. That left her two hours to spend with the kids.

Turning over, Diane watched her sister, still asleep in the twin bed beside her. She thanked God again that she had Em with them this week.

Trying to make as little noise as possible, Diane got out of the bed and pulled on her thin summer robe. Rummaging through her suitcase, she found the pair of terry-cloth slippers and put them on. Treading softly, she crossed the room and opened the door to the hallway. On her way to the bathroom, she noticed that the door to Michelle's room was ajar.

She knocked softly and poked her head through the doorway. "Michelle?" she called gently.

The room was empty, but it looked liked a tornado had swept through it. A suitcase lay open, its contents spilling over the sides. Clothes were strewn across the floor and unmade bed. Michelle's bottles of shampoos, conditioners, and creams were spread out over the dresser, and her CDs and DVDs lay in a jumbled mess on the night table. Diane shook her head and sighed. How had her daughter managed to wreak such havoc in such a short time?

And where was she?

Hoping that she wouldn't run into anyone but driven to go anyway, Diane started down the stairs. No one was in the lobby, or in the parlor. But Carlos and another man were in the dining room, arranging food and flowers on the buffet table.

"Excuse me," Diane said.

The men turned. Carlos smiled broadly. "Good morning, Ms. Mayfield."

"Diane. Please."

"Okay, Diane." Carlos turned in the direction of the other man. "Diane, this is my partner, Kip."

"Nice to meet you," Diane said as she pulled her robe closer around herself. "I'm not usually out prowling around a public place in my bathrobe, but I'm looking for my daughter."

"I haven't seen her yet this morning," said Carlos.

"Is she about thirteen or fourteen, brown hair, very thin?" asked Kip.

Diane nodded, wincing inwardly at the last description.

"Then I saw her leave about a half hour ago. She had shorts and sneakers on and had a Walkman with her. I just assumed that she was going for a run."

By the time Diane went back upstairs, showered, brushed her teeth, and returned to the room to dress, Emily was awake.

"Good morning, sleepyhead."

Her sister stretched out in the bed and sighed. "Oh, that felt good. If this is any indication of how the sleeping is going to be down here, I'm glad I came."

Diane pulled a black Donna Karan T-shirt over her head. "Want to come downstairs with me for some breakfast? I smelled something good cooking."

"Are the kids awake already?" Emily showed no signs of rising.

"Anthony is still sleeping, but Michelle's up and out already. I think she went for a run." Zipping up her white slacks, she added, "Em, can I ask you something?"

"What?"

"It's about Michelle." Diane swallowed. "Do you think she could have an eating disorder?"

Emily shifted her pillows and propped herself up. "God, Diane. I hadn't really thought about it."

Diane recounted her observations. The uneaten

garlic bread, the barely touched pizza, the loss of interest in what were once her favorite foods. "She's been exercising like crazy, too, and it looks to me like she's lost some weight."

Emily was silent for a moment as she considered her sister's words. When she finally answered, Diane felt a bit better.

"Yeah, all that might be true," Emily said. "But do you remember when you were that age? All the competition to be the prettiest and have the best figure? Heck, that never changes. I think Michelle could just be responding to the pressures of being a female in our society. Does that mean she has an eating disorder? I doubt it, Diane."

"God, I hope you're right, Em. I hope you're right."

CHAPTER 44

Wanting to get the local version of what was happening, Matthew stopped at Ocean Grove Stationery on Main Avenue to buy a copy of the *Asbury Park Press*. He especially needed to find out where Carly Neath had been babysitting the night she disappeared. That was an element they hadn't had time to pay attention to for the piece last night but something they'd definitely need for the *Hourglass* segment. The police had refused to provide that information at their news conference, but local reporters had their own sources—sources that a journalist just coming into town couldn't possibly match. Matthew was hoping that the *Asbury Park Press* reporter had done some of his work for him.

He stood on the sidewalk in front of the candy store and read the front-page article. Sure enough, it revealed that Carly had been babysitting for the Richey family, summer residents who lived in one of the tents on Bath Avenue. The information excited Matthew, because he knew that not only were the tents visually attractive but their story would be an interesting sidebar.

He continued to read, discovering that Carly also worked as a waitress at Nagle's Apothecary Café. That was the place on the corner of Main, not so far from the beach. He'd noticed it yesterday on his way back to the motel. It was within walking distance now. It was worth trying to see if he could talk with anyone who knew Carly.

A few minutes later, Matthew reached the café. There were small tables set up on the sidewalk, but he opted for the interior's air-conditioning. Scanning the room, he saw that all the tables were filled, but there was one seat open at the end of the counter. He slid onto the stool, next to a balding, middle-aged man.

"What'll it be?" asked the waitress.

"Some coffee, for starters, Anna," Matthew said, reading her name tag. "Black, no sugar. Then I'd like a couple of eggs, over easy, and whole wheat toast."

"Bacon?"

"Why not? Life is short."

The middle-aged man turned to look at him, leaving Matthew with the feeling he had said something wrong. Matthew smiled uncertainly.

"How ya doin'?" he asked the man.

"Fine." The man took a drink of orange juice. "You here on vacation?"

"No, but I wish I were. It's beautiful around here."

The man nodded as he reached into his pocket, pulled out a white business card, and handed it to Matthew. "I'm Larry Belcaro, Surfside Realty. If you're ever looking for a place in Ocean Grove or Asbury Park, I'm your man."

"Thanks, Larry," said Matthew, slipping the card in his pocket and seizing the opportunity to talk to a local. "So I guess you live around here?"

"Yep. Been in Ocean Grove for over twenty years."

"Family?"

Larry looked down at the counter, and Matthew was immediately sorry that he'd asked. "Not anymore," the man answered quietly.

Matthew's bacon and eggs arrived, relieving the awkwardness of the moment. He took a bite of his toast, folded his newspaper, and positioned it on a clear section of the counter. "This is some story, isn't it?" he asked, motioning with his fork in the direction of the newsprint.

Larry nodded. "Yeah, it's hard to believe that all this has been happening in our little town. It's usually so nice and quiet around here. You shouldn't think we have a high crime rate or anything."

Matthew shook his head, realizing that the salesman wanted Ocean Grove to be seen in the best possible light. "No, I wasn't thinking that at all."

The waitress came back, refilled their coffee cups, and left both checks on the counter. As Larry picked his up, Matthew spoke. "It says in the article the missing girl works here. Do you know her?"

Larry nodded. "She was a pretty little thing. Always bright and chipper when she waited on me. But I used to tease her that she should eat something herself. She was too thin if you ask me, just like Anna here." Larry nodded in the direction of their waitress as he laid her tip on the counter and maneuvered himself off the stool. "Well, gotta go. But remember, if you're ever in the market for some real estate, call me."

"Will do." Matthew smiled and watched Larry walk out the front door, noting that he had referred to Carly Neath entirely in the past tense.

CHAPTER 45

As Diane was going down the stairs, she met Michelle coming up. Her daughter's face was bright red, and brown strands had escaped the covered elastic band that pulled her hair back in a ponytail.

"Have a good run?"

"Yeah, it was fine."

"Where'd you go?"

"Up and down the boardwalk a couple of times."

Diane nodded. "I'm going down to the dining room to get something to eat. Want to come with me?"

"No, thanks. I want to go up and take a shower."

Diane's face fell.

"What now, Mom?"

"Listen, honey. I want to be able to spend some time with you. I have to go to work in about an hour, and I don't know when I'll be back. I just was hoping we could sit down together for a little while."

Michelle sighed heavily. "All right." Diane ignored the grudging tone in her daughter's voice.

When they entered the dining room, Diane noticed Sammy Gates sitting at a table by the window. At another time she would have forced herself to invite him to join them, but this morning she just waved, called a greeting, and led the way to a table in the corner on the opposite side of the room. Carlos came over right away, took their drink orders, and pointed to the buffet.

"Help yourself to as much as you want," he said. "If you want toast, just let me know and I'll make it in the back. But you must try the sticky buns. Kip bakes them, and they're absolutely divine."

"Shall we?" Diane asked her daughter.

The buffet table was laden with silver chafing dishes containing scrambled eggs, sausage, and home-fried potatoes. A napkin-lined wicker basket held blueberry muffins and mini bagels. There was a big crystal bowl full of granola ready to be scooped into flowered bowls and a pretty pitcher full of milk. The special sticky buns were displayed on a large round tray. Their aroma was intoxicating.

"Wow, this looks delicious," Diane said. Not knowing when she would get another chance to eat, she began helping herself to a bit of almost everything.

"Is that all you're going to have?" she asked, staring at the dollop of scrambled eggs and the lone bagel on Michelle's plate.

"That's all I want right now, Mom."

"Oh, come on, honey. You have to eat more than that," Diane urged.

"No, Mom, this is all I want."

They went back to their table, and Carlos brought Michelle's Diet Coke and Diane's iced tea.

"It's not good to drink soda so early in the day, honey."

Michelle rolled her eyes. "Stop nagging me, will you, Mom?"

Diane salted her eggs. "I'm not nagging you. I'm just a little worried about you, sweetheart, that's all."

Michelle took a sip of soda before answering. "You don't have to worry about me. I'm fine."

"Are you, Michelle? Are you really fine?" Diane searched her daughter's face.

"You mean about Daddy?"

"Partly," Diane said softly.

"What's the other part?"

Diane took a deep breath and then blurted it out.

"I'm worried about the way you've been eating, Michelle. I've noticed that you barely pick at your food, and I think you've lost some weight."

Michelle's face brightened. "You think I look thinner? Great."

"Honey, you didn't need to lose an ounce. You look wonderful."

"You're my mother. Of course you're going to say that."

Diane put down her fork. "No, I mean it, Michelle. You look just fine, in fact I think you could stand to gain a few pounds."

"No way." Michelle frowned.

"I'm not saying you have to put the weight you've lost back on, but I really think you shouldn't be trying to lose any more."

"You don't get it, Mom."

"Oh yes, I do. But I know that how thin we are isn't the thing we should be focusing on. It's not the most important thing."

Michelle sat back in her chair. "What, are you kidding me, Mom? I've seen you studying yourself in the full-length mirror in your bedroom. I've heard you worry about your weight all the time."

Diane felt slapped. Had she contributed to her daughter's obsession? "The reason I do is because the television camera makes you look heavier than you are. If I didn't have to be on TV all the time, I can assure you I wouldn't pay so much attention to my appearance."

"Sure, right." Michelle smiled smugly. "Do you mean to tell me that if you weren't on television, you wouldn't color your hair blond, or have your nails done, or buy nice clothes?"

"I don't follow you."

"You do all those things because you want to be attractive, Mom. It has nothing to do with being on television. You want to look good."

Diane thought about what her daughter was saying. "Yes, but I have to look good to make my living."

"And I have to be thin to be popular at school, to be in the A group, to make guys like me. You brought it up, so I'm telling you, Mom. That's just the way it is." Michelle folded her arms across her chest.

Diane wasn't going to let those be the last words. She reached across the table and took hold of her daughter's arm. "Oh, Michelle, honey. Don't you see? It's not what's on the outside that counts most. Sure, it's nice to be physically attractive. There's absolutely nothing wrong with that. But it's not healthy to be obsessed with your weight and how you look. There are so many more important things in life. Your character is what counts, the content of your mind and the goodness of your heart. Not the external things."

Michelle's eyes glazed over. Diane could tell her daughter wasn't buying it.

CHAPTER 46

Arthur had no shadow as he stood at the end of the boardwalk. The sun was directly above his head, beating down mercilessly. He looked out at all the people baking on the sand, blistering and risking heatstroke. And they called *him* crazy.

He jumped down onto the sand and trudged toward the water, fully aware of the stares. People were always looking at him, thinking him odd, grateful they weren't him. Arthur had gotten used to it.

Turning north, he left the more crowded beach of Ocean Grove behind in favor of the neglected sands of Asbury Park. No barrier separated one beach from the other, but the empty beer bottles, soda cans, and paper debris littering the Asbury Park beach distinguished it from the well-tended Ocean Grove sand just yards away.

The screeches and laughter of the children playing in the rolling surf grew fainter as Arthur distanced himself from the sun worshipers. He turned around to look back at them. They weren't paying attention to him anymore.

He tried to appear aimless as he plodded across the sand toward the old Casino, knowing that when he did it, he had to do it like lightning, in a flash. Just where the Casino jutted out farthest toward the ocean, there was about two feet of space between the sand and the giant concrete slab upon which the building stood. He cut gradually across the scorching sand, and then he dropped down on all fours and slithered forward on his belly into the darkness beneath the giant concrete slab.

It took all of three seconds. Arthur was confident that no one had seen him. No one ever did. It was dim and cool inside, a relief from the blinding brightness and heat of the beach. As he'd been taught for combat in Desert Storm, Arthur scurried, like a sand crab, deeper into the darkness.

CHAPTER 47

The camera crew waited on the sidewalk in front of Lavender & Lace while Diane and Matthew went into the shop to ask for permission to shoot the activity at the makeshift search headquarters. Once the consent was given, Sammy and Gary carried their gear inside, careful not to knock into the merchandise that crowded the store.

The storeroom was abuzz with activity. People were clustered around a giant map of the area, sipping coffee as they got their instructions on where to search. The copy machine whirred as it printed out flyers with Carly Neath's smiling face. At a long trestle table, a middle-aged man held a telephone receiver to his ear.

"That was the police," the man said as he hung up. "They say they're bringing in search dogs. That's more than they did for Leslie."

Audrey Patterson held her finger to her lip and shook her head. "Don't, Lou. This isn't the time."

Diane overheard the exchange and realized the man must be Leslie's father. She was about to introduce herself when the man rose from his chair and strode over to the doorway, coming face-to-face with a younger man who'd just arrived.

"Hello, Mr. Patterson," the younger man said in a low voice.

"What are you doing here?" Leslie's father demanded.

"I came to see what I could do to help."

"Oh, I see. You never showed up to search for Leslie, but you want to look for Carly. That's nice, Shawn. Haven't you done enough already?"

"Please, Mr. Patterson. Please understand. I'm sorry about Leslie. I just couldn't come."

"Couldn't come or wouldn't come?" Lou Patterson didn't wait for the answer. "You have a hell of a nerve showing your face around here, kid. First you dump my daughter, and when she disappears you're nowhere to be found. Now all of a sudden you want to help find another girl who had the misfortune to get involved with you. I know the cops are looking at you, Shawn. And you're here as the concerned boyfriend? What a joke."

"That's not true, Mr. Patterson."

"Don't tell me it's not true." Leslie's father's face reddened. "I can see right through you, and so can the police. I only wish Leslie could have seen through you too. Now get the hell out of here."

CHAPTER 48

The smell invaded the air, wafting up through Arthur's nostrils. It was a recognizable, distinctive smell. The odor that resulted from sickness, revulsion, or fear. He had known all of these.

Arthur wasn't sure if he wanted to investigate further. He had just come in to escape for a while, to get away to somewhere dark and cool and peaceful. He sat on the old bleacher, looked up at the hole in the auditorium ceiling, and tried to decide what to do. He could ignore it and leave, or he could follow the smell and see where it led.

He got up, thinking that it would be best to leave. Glass and pebbles crunched beneath his high-top sneakers as he walked across the bleachers, heading for the passageway back out to the beach. But as the smell grew stronger, Arthur found himself compelled to follow it. He stepped down to the auditorium floor and went toward the old refreshment stand. The odor pulled him closer.

Arthur poked his head behind the counter. In the dim

illumination from the hole in the ceiling, he could see a human form lying there. He stopped and waited to see if it moved. It didn't.

Nervously clearing his throat three times, Arthur inched forward. Spying the long, light hair, he forgot his reticence. He bent over the figure and rolled it over. Pulling off the blindfold that covered the eyes, he gasped. It was that pretty Carly Neath, Shawn's friend. As Arthur began to untie the gag around her mouth, he realized the smell was coming from the vomit soaking the cloth and covering Carly's cheeks.

She wasn't moving. Arthur shook her shoulders. He tried to clear her mouth and perform the resuscitation he had learned so long ago. But he couldn't get her to breathe on her own.

He had to get her out of here. He had to get her some help. Frantically, Arthur pulled at the sturdy plastic strips that bound Carly's ankles and held her wrists together. He felt at the birthmark on the inside of her limp wrist, searching in vain for a pulse.

CHAPTER 49

While Matthew and the crew stayed behind, capturing the images and sounds of the volunteers' search head-quarters, Diane followed the young man who had been ordered out of the Lavender & Lace storeroom by Leslie Patterson's father.

"Shawn. Shawn," she called after him.

He turned around and looked at her with bloodshot eyes. "Yes?" he said warily.

"Shawn, I'm Diane Mayfield with KEY News." She put out her right hand. As he automatically reached out to shake it, she added, "Would you be willing to talk with me?"

Shawn pulled his hand back and ran it through his auburn hair. Diane noticed that his nails were bitten to the quick.

"I don't think that would be a very good idea," he said. "Not in here, anyway." He looked uncomfortably around the store's display area. "Maybe we should go outside."

On the sidewalk, Diane spoke first. "That was pretty rough for you in there, wasn't it?"

Shawn nodded, squinting in the bright sun. "Yeah. I shouldn't expect Mr. Patterson to understand how terrible I feel about what happened to Leslie. But I couldn't get involved in the search for her. I just couldn't."

"Why not?" Diane asked gently.

"Look, I really shouldn't be talking to you. The police think I have something to do with Leslie's and Carly's disappearances. They don't think it's a coincidence that I happened to be dating both of them."

"It doesn't look good," Diane agreed. "Maybe it would be a good idea to get your side of the story out there, Shawn."

"No," he said, shaking his head. "I don't think I

should say anything on camera—at least not until I talk to my lawyer." He put the tip of his index finger to his mouth and tore at the ragged nail.

"All right, I understand," said Diane. "But how would it be if we talked off the record? You can tell me your side of things. To tell this story fairly, I need to know where you're coming from."

" 'Off the record' means you can't tell anyone what I say?"

"Not unless you decide to give me your permission."

Diane could see he was still uncertain. "Look, let's just start with some simple things. Like spelling your last name for me."

He complied, and she wrote it down in her notebook.

"And what do you do, Shawn?"

"I'm a graduate student, and I tend bar some nights at the Stone Pony to make money."

"What are you studying?"

"I'm working on my MSW."

"Social work?"

Shawn nodded.

"Admirable," Diane said. "And what do you want to do after you finish school?"

"Work with the mentally ill."

The wheels in Diane's mind sped. "Was that why you were attracted to Leslie Patterson, Shawn? Because she was troubled?"

He looked down at the sidewalk. "Maybe," he muttered. "I guess I didn't even realize it at first."

"Leslie was pretty needy, huh?"

"That's the understatement of the year." Shawn sighed heavily. "No matter how much attention I gave her, it was never enough. I thought I could help her, but I couldn't. I thought that if I made her feel secure, she would feel better about herself and start eating right. You'd think, with all the studying I've done, I'd have known better. I couldn't make Leslie well. She had to do that for herself."

"I thought she was in therapy," Diane said.

"She was. But I don't know what good it was doing. That therapist of hers had a helluva job, though. Anorexia wasn't Leslie's only problem."

Diane waited.

"Leslie was cutting herself. When I found that out, I couldn't take it anymore."

"So you broke up with her?" Diane asked.

"Yeah, I'm not proud of it, but I did. I had to get out of the relationship. It wasn't healthy. But I felt guilty about breaking up with her, believe me. And when Leslie disappeared, I didn't think she had been kidnapped at all. I thought she was hiding somewhere, just to get attention. My attention. That's why I didn't join the search. I didn't want to feed into her sickness."

"So what do you think now, Shawn? Now that Carly Neath is missing too?" Diane's eyes searched his face. "Do you still think Leslie was faking it?"

Shawn stopped to consider the question. "No. I guess

161

I don't. Carly is one of the most well-adjusted, happy girls I've ever met. I'm sure Carly isn't faking this, so maybe Leslie wasn't either."

CHAPTER 50

He was as angry with God as he was with himself, so Larry didn't bother going to church anymore. But that didn't mean he had no Sunday ritual. Every single week, after breakfast at Nagle's, he drove the five miles to St. Anne's Cemetery.

Larry parked the car, got out, and walked across the parched, brown grass, careful not to step where he estimated the bodies to be lying beneath the ground. Weathered granite headstones marked the final resting places of hundreds, all somebody's loved ones. Husbands, wives, sons, daughters. Acres and acres of sadness and heartache.

Jenna's and his wife's markers stood out from the others around them, still fresh and bright, the years of exposure to the elements yet to take place. Though Larry took some small comfort from the thought that the two people he loved were lying down there, side by side, the rage he felt at the injustice of their deaths trumped all other emotions.

He knelt on one knee and instinctively crossed himself, knowing as he did it was wrong to cloak himself in religious ritual while he had so much anger in his heart. He knew he should let go of his hatred of Owen Messinger, but he just couldn't do it and he shouldn't be expected to. That man had ruined all their lives.

Larry rubbed his hand over the granite gravestone, then traced Jenna's carved name with his finger as he whispered, "I promise you, honey. I swear. I'll make sure that Owen Messinger can't do to other girls what he did to you. I've warned him now, and if he doesn't stop on his own, I'm going to stop him."

CHAPTER 51

Leslie spent her morning doing her sit-ups and leg lifts, washing her hair, taking a shower, and dressing, killing time before leaving for Lavender & Lace. When she got to search headquarters, she was going to do whatever was asked of her to help find Carly Neath, even though Carly had stolen Shawn away.

She pulled on a pair of cotton capri pants, noticing that they were a little looser than the last time she'd worn them. It seemed like so long ago now, but it was only the week before last. Shawn had taken her to play miniature golf, and she'd thought they were having so much fun. But when they went out to get something to eat after the game, they'd gotten into another fight. Shawn had insisted that she eat; Leslie didn't want to. The next time they went out, Shawn told her he didn't want to see her anymore.

Even though she was devastated Shawn had broken things off, Leslie almost felt sorry for him now. Last night she had overheard her parents talking about him and how the police must be looking at him as a suspect in both her and Carly's disappearances. Her father had been especially angry, declaring Shawn a no-good SOB. Her mother had quieted her husband, saying that he should just be relieved to know their daughter had been telling the truth all along.

Leslie went downstairs and stopped in the kitchen, opening the refrigerator and taking out a couple of celery stalks. She was looking for her other flip-flop when the telephone rang.

"Leslie? It's Dr. Messinger. How are you?"

Leslie closed her eyes. "I'm fine."

There was a pause on the line. The kind of pause Leslie was used to in their sessions. The pause that meant Dr. Messinger was waiting for her to continue talking. Well, she wasn't going to fall for it this time.

Messinger gave in. "I just wanted to remind you about group tomorrow."

"I don't think I'm going to be able to make it this time, Dr. Messinger. You know, I'm just going back to work tomorrow and everything. I think it's better if I skip it this time."

"I don't think that's wise." His voice was calm and patient. "It's important that you come. You've just been through a very traumatic time. Come and let the group congratulate you on your survival."

"To tell you the truth, Dr. Messinger, I'm sick of

164

therapy. I don't think it's doing me any good. I want to try things on my own."

"We can talk about that when you come, Leslie. Four o'clock tomorrow. And remember, bring your stuffed animal."

"All right," said Leslie, already hating herself for giving in. "But this is the last time I'm coming."

It was as if the gods didn't want her to get to Lavender & Lace to help with the search for Carly. Leslie was standing on the porch locking the door when a police car pulled up at the curb. Chief Jared Albert himself, accompanied by another officer, got out of the vehicle and strode up the sidewalk. Leslie was pleased to see him take off his cap as a sign of respect when he reached her.

"Leslie, we have some questions to ask you," he said. "Your answers might help us find Carly Neath."

"Would you like to go in the house?" she asked. "It's so hot out here."

Chief Albert looked at the front door. "Are your parents home?" he asked.

"No, they're at the store with the search volunteers."

"It's just as well we talk out here on the porch then," he said. He might believe Leslie Patterson's story now that Carly Neath had gone missing too, but he still wasn't sure how stable she was. He didn't need to take any chances with a young woman who could falsely accuse the police of improper behavior. No, it was better to stay right here on the porch for everyone to see.

Leslie took her place in the rocker, while Albert and the younger officer sat side by side on the wicker sofa.

"We need more details about what happened during your abduction, Leslie," said the chief.

"I already told everything I remember when I was in the hospital," she replied. "What else do you want to know?"

"We'd like to know more about the dancing you described. There was no music playing?"

"No, just the sound of the ocean."

"You said you were blindfolded. But could you feel anything?"

She closed her eyes and tried to get a mental image. "I felt the man was wearing a nylon jacket of some kind. I could hear it swishing as his arms moved."

"Anything else?"

"I'm pretty sure he was wearing gloves too."

"Do you think they were latex, the kind a dentist wears?" asked Chief Albert.

"No, I think they were leather. I could smell the leather."

"Thank you for your cooperation with this, Leslie."

"That's okay," she answered. "I want to do anything I can to help. I'm on my way to the volunteer search headquarters now."

"Can we drop you off?" offered Chief Albert.

"No thanks. I'll walk." As she stood on the porch and watched the officers get back into their car, Leslie let out a sigh of relief. The police finally believed her.

CHAPTER 52

They decided to go back to the Starving Artist for lunch. After a ten-minute wait, they were seated at a table for four. Diane, Matthew, and Gary ordered club sandwiches, while Sammy, ever happy to take advantage of the KEY News expense account, ordered the more expensive crab cakes, a side of beer-battered onion rings, and a slice of cheesecake.

"What are you, begging for a heart attack?" said Matthew.

"Don't worry about me. I've got good genes," Sammy boasted. "No heart disease in my family."

"Ever hear of not tempting fate?" Matthew asked, to which Sammy only smiled smugly.

While they waited for their food, Diane recounted her conversation with Shawn Ostrander, giving his explanation of his relationship with Leslie Patterson and why he'd had to break up with her.

"I don't know," she said, stirring her iced tea. "I just can't picture this guy abducting women. He seems so earnest and sincere."

"Those are the ones you have to watch out for." Sammy sneered.

Diane ignored the remark.

"What about Carly?" asked Matthew. "Shawn must know that it looks bad for him that both of the missing women have been his girlfriends."

Usually quiet, Gary spoke up. "I sure wouldn't want to be in *his* shoes."

"Me neither," Sammy agreed.

After they'd finished eating and were waiting for Sammy to wolf down his dessert, Matthew pulled out the newspaper and showed Diane the section about Carly's babysitting for a tent family named Richey on Bath Avenue. "I think we should head over there next," he said. "Get pictures of the tent, see if someone will talk to us."

"Each one of these is cuter than the next. They're all so charming," said Diane as they walked down Bath Avenue. The tents, with their colorful striped awnings and hanging baskets full of summer flowers, created a scene from another world. A simpler, safer world, where young women didn't have to think about being abducted in the dark of night.

Sammy and Gary went about shooting the street and the various tents, knowing it was important to give the video editor as many choices as possible for when he or she put the piece together at the Broadcast Center. Meanwhile, Diane and Matthew tried to find someone to tell them which was the Richeys' tent. But the tent porches were empty, their usual residents driven either inside or away by the afternoon heat.

"I guess we'll have to start knocking," said Diane.

There was no answer at the first two tents they tried. At the next, a little blond girl opened the screen door.

"Hello. Is your mother or father home?" Diane asked.

"My daddy's out, but my mommy's here." The child stood staring at Diane.

"Could I speak with your mother, please?"

The child let go of the screen door and turned away. "Mommy," she yelled into the tent. "There's someone here."

"Who is it?"

"I don't know."

Diane was about to tell the child who she was when the mother came to the door. Diane thought the woman flinched slightly as she introduced Matthew and herself. "We're looking for the Richey family's tent."

"This is it. I'm Helen Richey. May I help you?"

"Oh, great," said Diane. "I suppose you can guess why we're here, Mrs. Richey. The article in the *Asbury Park Press* said Carly Neath was working here the night she disappeared."

Helen Richey turned and called back into the tent. "Girls, I'll be out on the porch." Closing the door behind her, she indicated that Diane and Matthew could take seats in the wicker chairs. "I don't want the children to hear anything," she said.

"Of course not," said Diane.

"We were hoping you could tell us about what happened that night," said Matthew, looking over Helen's shoulder to see if he could spot the camera crew and signal them to come over.

"We've told the police everything," said Helen, twisting her slim gold wedding band as she decided to corroborate her husband's story. "Carly babysat for the girls for about four hours. We got home after eleven o'clock. We paid her, and she left. It was a night like so many others when she's worked for us."

"So Carly went home on her own?" asked Diane. "No one walked her?" She tried to keep her tone from sounding accusatory. But she could sense the tension in Helen Richey's voice when she answered.

"Carly lives just a few blocks away. She was insistent that she walk home on her own. My husband and I thought it would be safe enough." She bit her lower lip, and tears welled in her eyes. "We made a mistake in letting her walk home alone, and if something terrible has happened to Carly, we'll never forgive ourselves."

CHAPTER 53

The tops of his feet were red, Anthony noticed as he sloshed through the salty water lapping over the sand. He supposed he should go back and slather on more of the sunscreen in his aunt Emily's bag, but he didn't want to. He had no desire to hang out with his aunt and his sister. He wanted to be by himself. He was still bummed out over missing his chance to go to the

Grand Canyon. This boring beach vacation wasn't cutting it.

He took a picture of a sand castle, deserted by its architects, before he kicked the structure over. Then he bent down to pick up a piece of sea glass and continued his walk up the beach. Anthony watched the kids on boogie boards surfing in the waves, deciding that he was going to get his mother to buy him one of his own. Over the ocean, a windsurfer, tethered to a motorboat in the water below, glided through the air. Maybe he could get his mother to let him give that a try too.

She owed him. Big time. Even though he knew, deep down, his mother was doing everything she could to make him and Michelle happy, and he knew he should appreciate it and stop giving her a hard time, he was ticked off. He had bragged to all his friends about the cool trip he'd be taking this summer. Now, when school started and they found out he hadn't gone, they'd say he'd been full of crap. Coming on top of his father's going to jail, Anthony couldn't afford one more thing to make him look bad.

Maybe he could figure out a way to put a different spin on things. But what could possibly happen in Ocean Grove that would impress his friends? His mother would kill him if he tried to get involved in the search for that girl. But it would be neat if he could find her. That would be so cool. He'd probably be on the news.

"Anthony. Annnnthoneeee."

He turned around. Emily was standing down the beach, waving her arms, calling him like he was a little kid. Resigned, he started to trudge back through the water. He hadn't gone far when he saw the man dressed in army fatigues slip from beneath the concrete that surrounded the big round brick building. Anthony stared as the man planted himself in the sand and curled up in a fetal position. He snapped a picture before he hurried down the beach.

CHAPTER 54

God forgive her. She'd made it sound as if Jonathan had been with her when Carly was paid for babysitting that night—that he was in the tent with his wife when Carly insisted on walking home by herself. Helen had misled Diane Mayfield and the KEY News producer just now, as she had stood by when Jonathan lied to the police yesterday. She prayed that God would forgive her.

In order to be forgiven, Helen knew she had to be truly repentant. God could see into her heart, so He would know that she was truly sorry. But He must also see that she didn't know what else to do. Jonathan was her husband, the father of her children, and there was no way she was going to point a finger at him.

Helen went back into the tent and admired her children's artwork as they colored at the kitchen table.

"That's beautiful, Hannah. I think we should hang that one up. Yours too, Sarah."

She taped the crayoned seascapes onto the refrigerator, knowing that Jonathan would be back soon from his run on the beach. Fueled by suspicion and fear, she went to the bedroom dresser to find her husband's wallet. Inside the leather billfold there was a couple hundred dollars in cash to get them through the week, a Visa and MasterCard, a new high-tech New Jersey driver's license, and a white business card. "Surfside Realty" was stamped across it in blue block letters. Helen turned the card over and read the handwritten notation. "Thursday, August 18. 4:00."

It didn't make sense. Jonathan couldn't have had an appointment to look at real estate on Thursday afternoon. He hadn't even been here on Thursday. Jonathan hadn't come down to the shore until Friday.

CHAPTER 55

"I'm always going to love this town," said Carlos, taking his partner's hand as they and their real estate agent walked along the near-empty boardwalk. "Asbury Park issued us our marriage license."

"Well, you and Kip would be very smart to buy something here as soon as you can," said Larry, pulling off his tie in the heat. "The prices have already escalated dramatically, and now that the billion-dollar development project has the green light, you can be sure things are only going to get more expensive."

"Yeah," Kip agreed. "Once they pour that money into developing all this empty space on the waterfront, Asbury Park should really return to life."

"I hope to God they don't ruin things by tearing down all the interesting and historic places." Carlos frowned. "I'm still sick about the Palace. Who'd have thought a wrecker's ball would demolish the nation's oldest indoor amusement park? It was on the National Register of Historic Places and everything. I'll never understand what passes for progress."

They slowed as they reached the decaying old Casino, with its wind-scarred copper filigree work. "You haven't heard that they're going to tear this place down, have you, Larry?" Kip asked. "I'd die if they destroyed this place. It's my favorite building in Asbury Park."

"Well, I know there's a few preservation groups who say they'll never let it be torn down," said Larry. "But I guess you can never say never."

The three men stood looking out toward the ocean and discussed the fact that gays and lesbians had found a tolerant community in Asbury Park, a town grateful for the help these newcomers were giving to its revival.

"Asbury Park is what South Beach, Florida, was twenty years ago," said Carlos. "We want to get in on the turnaround."

Kip agreed. "Yes. We love the way we have been

welcomed in Ocean Grove, and we're thrilled with our inn. We already have reservations for next season. But by the end of the year, we'll be finished with our renovations on the Dancing Dunes. We'll be ready to take on another project."

"Well, should we start looking at what's available now?" asked Larry. "Even though you don't think you're ready to buy quite yet, you can start educating yourself on the Asbury Park market. I have a couple of listings right now that, with some tender loving care, could be fabulous bed-and-breakfast places."

"Sounds good," said Kip. "And, Larry? Before I forget. Can I have a few of your business cards? I have some friends who are interested in finding something in Asbury Park as well."

As Larry took out his billfold and handed over the white cards, a police car skidded to a stop in front of the Casino.

CHAPTER 56

A small crowd gathered in front of the old Casino as the police led the man from the beach.

"It's going to be all right, pal," said one of the officers. "We're going to get you some help."

The man stumbled through the sand, flanked by two policemen, who struggled to keep him walking. His camouflage shirt was open, his hair mussed. He stared straight ahead, his eyes glassy. Arthur didn't utter a sound.

CHAPTER 57

They searched for as long as the light held out, knocking on doors, looking under the boardwalk and up and down the streets. Since it was church property, the Ocean Grove Camp Meeting Association gave permission for the volunteer search parties to look under every tent on its grounds. Tenters themselves readily opened their doors, sure that Carly Neath was not going to be found in their tiny canvas homes.

It was just after nine o'clock when everyone returned to Lavender & Lace and called off their search for the day, not knowing where they could possibly look tomorrow.

CHAPTER 58

When it had been dark for a few hours and it came time for the second dance, Carly's blindfold was off. Her gag was gone too, though her hands and feet were still bound.

Behind the deserted refreshment counter inside the

Casino, the beam from the flashlight illuminated Carly's lifeless face. Her mouth hung open. Fine blue veins showed beneath the translucent skin of her eyelids. Her cheeks and beautiful golden hair were matted with vomit.

This wasn't the way it was supposed to happen. It was supposed to go off just like the last time.

The yellow beam searched the littered ground, finding the discarded blindfold and gag. The rags were tied back in place, just as they had been the last time. But now, it would be different. The young woman the guard found this time would be dead. There was no sense in holding her for the full three days. The police would likely be able to figure out that Carly had not survived even two days in captivity.

MONDAY
AUGUST 22

CHAPTER 59

Diane awoke to the sound of her ringing cell phone. She felt on the bedside table for her watch. In the early morning light, she was barely able to see that it was only six o'clock.

"Hello," she answered groggily.

"Diane. It's Matthew. You've got to get up."

"What?" She rubbed at her eyes.

"Meet me at the police station. A satellite truck is on its way down, and you have a seven-twenty live shot for *KEY to America*."

Diane sat upright, trying to focus as Matthew continued talking.

"Carly Neath has been found, Diane. She's dead."

By the time Diane arrived at the police station, Matthew had written a script for her. Gary Bing recorded her narration and ran with the tape to the satellite truck that had just arrived from New York

City. The narration was fed to the Broadcast Center to be edited with various video elements that had already been fed in for Diane's *Evening Headlines* piece along with video recorded yesterday at Lavender & Lace and some of the tent shots taken on Bath Avenue. Meantime, Sammy Gates set up the gear to record the police press conference and transmit Diane's live portion of the report.

"The police said they would have a presser at seven o'clock," said Matthew, looking at his watch. "It's seven-oh-five. We better figure out what you're going to say if they don't talk in time."

Diane looked down, appearing to study the ground as she tried to compose what she would say when Harry Granger tossed to her from the studio in New York. The minutes ticked away, and still no police spokesperson came out to address the hastily assembled media.

Gary returned from the satellite truck and outfitted Diane with a wireless microphone and a tiny plastic earpiece. Once she inserted the earpiece, she could hear directions from the control room and whatever Harry Granger would ask her from the *KEY to America* studio.

"Five minutes, Diane," the warning voice came.

She gave the thumbs-up signal to Sammy's camera lens, knowing her image was flowing to the receivers at the Broadcast Center. She switched her cell phone to vibrate so it couldn't ring during the live shot.

"Let's have a mike check, Diane, please."

"Testing. One, two, three, four, five. Five, four, three, two, one."

She turned to check the empty podium set up on the sidewalk in front of the police station.

"Two minutes, Diane."

She pulled a mirror out of her purse, reapplied her lipstick, and smoothed her hair.

"One minute."

She could hear the story before hers wrapping up. Next she heard Harry Granger's deep voice introducing her. Diane swallowed as she waited for the toss.

"KEY News Correspondent Diane Mayfield is in Ocean Grove, New Jersey, with the story. Diane?"

"Good morning, Harry," she began, her face somber. "Already in the grip of a record heat wave, this small beach community is now gripped by terror and fear— fear that there is a murderer on the loose. Early this morning, the body of twenty-year-old Carly Neath was discovered on the grounds of the Ocean Grove Camp Meeting Association—the same place where another young woman was found Friday morning after she had been missing for three days. Leslie Patterson was alive; Carly Neath, who never returned home after a babysitting job Friday night, wasn't as lucky."

At that point, the control room switched to the edited video package. For the next minute and a half, Diane listened through the earpiece to her own voice narrating the story that was being fed out to the entire

KEY network. Matthew's script covered all the bases, leading with Carly's disappearance after babysitting at one of the tents, talking about the townwide search that had followed the search for Leslie Patterson just days before. The script said local police had suspected Leslie Patterson of faking her own abduction, but with the disappearance of a second victim, now found dead, the investigation had taken another turn.

Diane knew the package was almost over. The camera would be coming back to her. She listened for the last words she had recorded. "The outcue is: 'mortal danger that lurks in Ocean Grove,'" came the voice in her ear.

She heard the closing words, waited a beat, and began speaking into the camera. "A police spokesperson is expected to come out any moment, Harry, to give us more details on the situation. Authorities have their hands full here. This is the height of the vacation season, and this town has almost twice the population it has in the winter months. That's a lot of frightened folks, Harry, and they want to feel safe again."

"What about Leslie Patterson, the young woman who was thought to have cried wolf?" the anchor asked. "She must take some comfort that people believe her now."

"We talked with Leslie this weekend, Harry. Of course, that was before Carly Neath was found. But Leslie said that was the worst part of an ordeal which included being held against her will for three days and nights and forced to dance, blindfolded, with her abductor. Worse than anything she'd been through, she said, had been the fact that people thought she was lying about it all."

Within moments of her signing off, Diane's cell phone vibrated.

"Nice piece."

She recognized the voice and winced.

"Just make sure you get exclusives for us. I don't want the day-of-air broadcasts to rob *Hourglass* of its thunder."

"Don't worry, Joel. There's plenty of misery to go around down here." Diane shook her head and rolled her eyes at Matthew. "Though this isn't the story we thought it was going to be, Joel. You sent me down here to cover a girl who cried wolf. Now it looks like we've got a young woman who was telling the truth and a killer on the loose."

"Not to worry." Joel's voice had a twisted lilt to it. "This could work out even better. Give our *Hourglass* broadcast another dimension."

"You mean . . ."

"I mean," Joel interrupted, "we already have the stories about the girls who really *did* cry wolf. Yours can focus on what it's like to be telling the truth and have no one believe you."

CHAPTER 60

Owen Messinger spooned cornflakes into his mouth as he watched Diane Mayfield on the television screen. He was going to have his work cut out for him with Leslie when she came for group therapy today—that is, *if* she came for group therapy.

If she had already seen herself as unfairly persecuted by everyone who hadn't believed her, her story getting national attention would only create further psychological issues for her to address. If Leslie had ever craved attention, she was certainly getting it now.

Stashing the cereal bowl in the kitchen sink, Owen took a can of cat food from the pantry and emptied its contents into the aluminum bowl on the floor. "Okay, Cleo, I'm leaving your food out, baby," he called. "Daddy's gonna be home late tonight."

He exited through the kitchen door, forgetting that he had left his cell phone recharging on the counter. He got into his black Volvo and adjusted the air-conditioning as high as it would go. Another scorcher was on the way.

It was a short drive to the office. When Owen pulled into the parking lot, he noticed two police cruisers parked near the entrance of the professional building. He parked the car in his reserved space, went directly into the building, and took the elevator to the third floor.

The door to his office was wide open.

"What's going on here?" Owen asked as he surveyed the overturned furniture in the reception area.

"Oh, Dr. Messinger," said Christine with relief. "I've been trying to reach you, but there was no answer on your cell. This is what I found when I came in." His assistant made a sweeping gesture at the disarray.

Owen looked past her, through the doorway to his office. The police officers were taking stock of the chaos in the room. "Can you tell if anything's missing?" asked one of them.

Taking his key ring from his pocket, Owen unlocked his desk drawers and checked each one. "Nothing has been touched here, thank goodness," he said.

"How about anywhere else? Anything missing?"

Owen looked over at the bookcase and saw the gaping space where his patient binders used to be. All of his treatment notes were gone.

CHAPTER 61

"Leslie. If you're going to go to work today, you have to get up."

Hearing her mother's shrill voice call up the stairs, Leslie groaned and turned over in her bed. She was still tired and didn't want to get up.

"I'm not kidding, Leslie. If you don't hurry, you won't have time for breakfast."

That's fine by me, thought Leslie as she rubbed her eyes. She lay on her back, staring up at the ceiling and the glow-in-the-dark plastic stars she had affixed there a good ten years ago. No wonder she was depressed. This was a kid's room, not a woman's. But if she had any hope of getting away from her parents' nagging and treating her like a child, she had to have an income of her own.

She forced herself to get out of bed, her bare feet landing on one of the hooked rugs her mother was so proud of making. Pale pink rosettes sprinkled the cream-colored background. Leslie looked from the rug to the pink walls and the white furniture painted with clusters of tiny flowers and made a vow. When she got a place of her own, there would be none of this frilly, girlie stuff.

She took off the T-shirt and gym shorts she'd slept in and stood before the mirror. As she turned from side to side, examining her body from different angles, Leslie promised herself she was going to eat as little as she possibly could today. That would be no small feat with her mother and Larry Belcaro watching her like hawks.

In the shower, the warm needles of water pounded against her tightly stretched skin. The towel felt rough against her back as she dried herself. Running the toothbrush around her mouth, she liked the way the white paste made her teeth look brighter.

She chose a short, brown cotton skirt and peach-colored blouse to wear for her first day back in the office, in part to please Larry. He always complimented her when she wore peach. He said it made her brown eyes look especially warm and pretty.

"Leslie. When are you going to get down here?"

"I'll be right there, Mom."

Spinning in front of the mirror again and sucking in her stomach and cheeks, Leslie wasn't satisfied with her appearance, but she couldn't do anything more than she already planned not to do.

Audrey Patterson scooped a large serving spoon of scrambled eggs onto her daughter's plate, followed by three strips of bacon and a buttered English muffin.

"Orange or pineapple juice, Leslie?"

"Orange, please."

As her mother turned her back to go to the refrigerator, Leslie ripped off a piece of her muffin, snatched a strip of bacon from her plate, and dropped them into the canvas tote bag she'd carefully lined with wax paper the night before and positioned on the floor next to her chair. As Audrey poured the juice into her daughter's glass, Leslie noticed her mother's eyes scanning her plate. Leslie slipped her fork under the scrambled eggs and put some in her mouth.

"Stop looking at me while I eat, will you, Mom? How many times have I told you how much I hate it when you do that?"

Audrey bit her lower lip. "I'm sorry, honey. I guess I don't even realize that I'm doing it. I just want to make sure you're eating."

"Well, you're only making things worse. It makes me nervous." Leslie put down her fork and sat back in her chair.

"All right. All right. I'll stop watching you."

Audrey went to the sink, squirted in some liquid detergent, and turned on the water. With her back to her daughter, she scoured the frying pan while Leslie deposited the rest of the bacon and half of the muffin in the tote bag. She knew well enough that if everything disappeared from her plate, her mother wouldn't believe she had eaten it all. By moving around the eggs and leaving a bit of muffin, she could get away from the table with her mother thinking she'd had enough for breakfast when in fact she'd consumed only a mouthful of egg and a few sips of orange juice.

"All right, I'm done." Leslie pushed back her plate. "I can't eat any more. I've got to get going."

Her mother turned from the sink, her eyes sweeping Leslie's plate and then searching her daughter's face. "Leslie, I have to tell you about something before you go."

"What?" Leslie asked cautiously.

"I had the news on before you came down for breakfast, honey, but I didn't want to tell you before you'd eaten."

"Tell me what?"

Audrey sat down across the table and reached out to

take hold of her daughter's arm. "Carly Neath was found at the Beersheba Well early this morning."

"Good," said Leslie, her face brightening. "Now everyone will totally believe me."

Audrey looked down at her lap.

"I didn't mean that was the most important thing, Mom," Leslie added hastily. "I'm glad they found Carly."

Audrey looked up again. There were tears in her eyes.

"What, Mom? What is it?"

"Carly is dead, sweetheart."

Leslie was silent.

"Leslie, honey, are you all right?"

"Yeah, I'm fine. I just don't know what to say. . . . Except I guess that could have been me. I realize how lucky I am, Mom." She picked up her tote bag and started for the door but stopped. "I forgot Lee Lee," she said. "I need her for group today. Dr. Messinger wants us to bring in our favorite childhood stuffed animal."

She ran back upstairs to her room and pulled the tattered teddy bear from its spot on the bookcase. Then she carefully lifted the wax paper lining from her tote, wrapped up the remains of her breakfast, and put it back inside the bag to discard later. She placed her beloved Lee Lee on top.

CHAPTER 62

Why hadn't he gotten that lawyer's beeper number or something? Shawn's heart pounded, and he could feel the heat in his cheeks as he hung up the telephone. The news, all over national television, that Carly's body had been found left Shawn feeling panicked. Leslie had disappeared, but Carly was actually dead. Both were his girlfriends, and the police suspected him. Before it was for kidnapping; now it could be for murder.

He was also ashamed. The fear that the police were going to come and drag him away superseded any emotion he felt over Carly's death. At the end of the day, he was just like so many others, wasn't he? Concerned primarily with his own well-being.

Shawn paced back and forth in the small living room of his apartment. He had to calm down, had to try to think rationally. The public defender would return his call and tell him what to do.

The ringing of the telephone cut the air. Thank God, the lawyer was calling back already. Shawn sprang for the receiver.

"Hello?"

"Shawn Ostrander, please."

"Speaking." It must be a secretary or receptionist calling. The lawyer would surely be on the line in a second.

"This is Jersey Shore University Medical Center calling. We have a patient, an Arthur Tomkins, admitted here. He has your name in his wallet as the person to notify."

"Is Arthur all right?" Shawn asked automatically.

"He's in stable condition. But you'll have to speak with the doctor for more details."

Shawn's chest tightened. He didn't want to be bothered with Arthur right now. He needed to concentrate on what he was going to do to get himself out of this nightmare.

"Mr. Ostrander?"

What kind of person was he? If Arthur needed him, he had to go to the poor man. He had to do the right thing. Besides, the police would be watching him. He should go about his business as though there was nothing amiss. In an instant, Shawn committed himself.

"Please tell Mr. Tomkins I'll be there as soon as I can."

CHAPTER 63

Chief Albert came out to apologize and say the press conference would be postponed until ten o'clock. At 10:00, he came out to promise he'd have something for the media at 11:30. Finally, at noon, he emerged from the tiny police station and stood behind the wooden podium, ready to make the announcement. The KEY satellite truck fed the video and audio to the Broadcast Center for use on the local news noon broadcast.

"Due to the urgency of this situation, an autopsy has already been performed on the body of twenty-year-old Carly Neath. The county medical examiner's office has determined that Ms. Neath died of asphyxiation."

"She was suffocated?" Diane called out.

Chief Albert consulted his notes before answering. "She choked on her own vomit."

"So she wasn't murdered?" asked the *Asbury Park Press* reporter.

"We don't know that," answered the policeman. "This is an ongoing investigation. But I can say, under New Jersey law, when someone abducts another person and that person dies during the abduction, the kidnapper would be considered responsible."

"So that means you think there is someone else out there who is responsible for Carly's death?" another reporter pressed.

"I didn't say that." There was annoyance in the officer's voice. "I can tell you that we are looking at every possibility." Chief Albert glanced in Diane's direction again.

"Of course the police understand that the community is extremely anxious about this case, Chief." Diane spoke in a measured tone. "They're terrified there's a killer on the loose in Ocean Grove. What would you tell them to alleviate their fears?"

"I'd tell them that the police are on top of the situation. That's all I'm going to say at this point, though we might have something more for you later today." With that, Chief Albert spun around and went back inside the station.

CHAPTER 64

With the sun so harsh she couldn't let her girls outside, and with all the tension and anxiety in town, Helen Richey finally agreed to allow a television set into the tent. She asked Jonathan to go out and buy one, only to have him remind her he already had one in the trunk of the car. He happily set it up.

While her daughters sat at the kitchen table eating tuna sandwiches, Helen sat in the front room of the tent, watching the clips of the police news conference on the WKEY noon news, careful to keep the volume low so the girls wouldn't hear. She saw Diane Mayfield and listened to her question about what could be done to alleviate the town's fears. When Chief Albert responded that the police were on top of the situation and might have more information later in the day, Helen shivered despite the warm air in the tent.

Carly Neath, that sweet girl, was dead. What if Jonathan had something to do with it? What if her husband had followed the young woman as she walked home Friday night? And what if Jonathan had also been involved in Leslie Patterson's disappearance last week?

Helen switched off the television, sat back down on the wicker chair, and tried to concentrate. The Surfside Realty business card she'd found in Jonathan's wallet indicated he'd had an appointment in Ocean Grove last Thursday afternoon. If that was true, why hadn't he told her about it? And if Jonathan was in town on Thursday, that meant he could have been the one who left Leslie Patterson tied up at the Beersheba Well gazebo in the middle of the night.

Where was he now, she wondered, as she got up, walked over to the screen door, and opened it. Helen looked up the street to see if he was coming back from his walk to the hardware store. He was forever doing errands, and in her heart, Helen suspected her husband was looking for reasons to get out of the tent and away from her and the kids.

Her mind raced. What if, somehow, Jonathan had cracked under the pressure of her demands that they live in a way he detested? That would make her partly responsible for what had happened to Carly and Leslie Patterson. She couldn't live with that.

Helen went inside. "Finished with lunch, girls?" she called as she strode resolutely toward the back of the tent. As soon as Jonathan got back from town, she was going to encourage him to get out the big umbrella and take the kids to the beach. Then she would be free to do what she had to do.

CHAPTER 65

Larry insisted on switching the phones over to the answering service, locking up the office, and taking Leslie to lunch. He decided against Nagle's or the Starving Artist, knowing that the locals would be gossiping about the Carly Neath tragedy and staring at Leslie. Instead, he drove around Wesley Lake to Asbury Park and the Italian restaurant that had been Jenna's favorite before his daughter obsessed about every morsel she put in her mouth.

For Larry, it was a painful hour as he watched Leslie eat very little of her salad. He knew better than to comment. He had learned that much at least when they were dealing with Jenna's problem.

"I'm so glad that you've come back to work, Leslie," he said as they waited for the check. "That's right where you should be. It's good to keep busy."

Leslie nodded and spoke softly. "You know, Larry, those three days were very, very scary. I have never been so afraid in my life. But when I was tied up and there all by myself, I found myself thinking about how messed up my whole life is."

Larry leaned forward to listen more closely.

"Now that I have another chance, I've been thinking about getting my real estate license."

"That would be super, Leslie." His weathered face

beamed. "You know I'll help you any way I can."

"I know you will," she said.

They drove back to the office, chatting about where Leslie could take the real estate licensing course and how difficult the state exam was. As Larry pulled into his parking space, they noticed that a woman was waiting at the front door. He hurried up to meet her, apologizing that she had been forced to wait outside in the heat.

"That's all right," said the honey-haired woman. "I just got here a little while ago."

"I'm Larry Belcaro." He extended his hand. "And this is my assistant, Leslie Patterson."

The woman shook Larry's hand, but her eyes stared at Leslie. "Helen Richey," she said.

Leslie took her seat at the desk near the door and picked up a magazine while Larry ushered the woman into his office.

"What is it you're looking for?" Larry asked. "Do you want to rent or buy?"

"Well, actually, neither," said the woman.

"Oh, you have a place to sell." He uncapped his pen. "Is it here in Ocean Grove?"

"No, it's not that either." Helen looked uncomfortable as she zipped open her purse and pulled out a small white card. "I'm trying to find out about this." She handed the card across the desk. "You see, I found it with my husband's things, and I wanted to ask if he had an appointment with you last week."

Larry looked at both sides of the card. "Let's see,"

196

he mused. "Last Thursday at four o'clock. I don't think so." He opened the appointment book on his desk. "No, that's right. I had a closing last Thursday. I didn't show any real estate that afternoon."

CHAPTER 66

"God, now *Evening Headlines* wants a piece for tonight." Matthew snapped his cell phone shut. "I tried to talk them into sending down one of their own producers and another correspondent, but they want you."

"I'd be flattered if I didn't know how short-staffed they are in August. It's me by default," Diane said. "Does Joel know?"

"Yep," Matthew replied. "Range Bullock talked to him, one executive producer to another."

Diane smiled. "I can just imagine that conversation, Joel reminding him again and again how much Range was going to owe him."

"Yeah, and we're the currency," Matthew declared, uncapping his pen and flipping open his notebook. "We might as well get to it. The only new video we have is the police presser this afternoon."

"And we can only hope they are going to say something else before airtime," Diane added.

"Range said he'd like us to try to give the flavor of the town, let the viewers see and feel Ocean Grove, get some reaction from people on the street. Do you want to go over to Nagle's, where Carly worked, and see if we can get reaction from people who knew her?" Matthew asked.

"Sounds like a plan," Diane agreed.

CHAPTER 67

He hated the smell of hospitals. Shawn tried not to inhale, listening to the squeak of his tennis shoes against the linoleum floor. *What a silly thing to focus on,* he thought as he walked down the long hallway. *You could be accused of kidnapping and murder—and you're wrinkling your nose at the scent of disinfectant.*

Shawn felt slightly better, though, since the public defender had called him back. The attorney said that the police would already have arrested Shawn if they'd had enough to connect him to Leslie's and Carly's abductions. The lawyer assured him that unless there was physical evidence or an eyewitness who tied him to the young women's disappearances, it was highly unlikely he could be convicted of anything. Just the fact that he had dated two women who had disappeared didn't make him a kidnapper or a killer. Shawn was holding on tight to those words.

The door to the hospital room was open. It was a double room, but the bed closer to the door was empty. Shawn treaded quietly toward the bed on the other side of the curtain.

"Arthur?" he whispered.

He opened his eyes and turned toward Shawn, his hair getting more disheveled as it rubbed against the pillow. Arthur's usually tanned skin looked almost ashen against the faded cotton hospital gown.

"How you doin', buddy?" Shawn asked.

Arthur didn't answer.

"What's wrong, Arthur? You can tell me, man," Shawn urged.

"He hasn't said a word since they brought him in here."

Shawn jumped at the woman's voice.

"Sorry, I didn't mean to startle you. I'm Dr. Varga," she said as she walked around the bed and reached for Arthur's wrist.

"I'm Shawn Ostrander."

"A relative?"

"No, a friend." There was no point in getting into the long story of how his association with the mentally ill man had started as a research project. Arthur had become more than that. "His relatives don't have anything to do with him anymore."

The doctor nodded.

"What's wrong with him?" Shawn asked.

"Nothing physically, but he's not talking. When the police brought him in, they filled us in on his mental status."

"Yeah, Arthur is pretty well known around town."

Shawn smiled crookedly.

The doctor scribbled a notation on the chart. "Fortunately, he had his meds in his jacket pocket. We can't be sure if he was taking them before he got here, but he's getting them now."

"When will you let him go home?" Shawn asked.

"That depends," answered Dr. Varga. "But I would suspect there is no rush, is there?"

Shawn shook his head, thinking of the sad little room in the tired boardinghouse that Arthur called home. "No, there isn't any rush at all," he said.

The doctor patted Arthur's arm before leaving the room. Shawn sat down and held a one-sided conversation about the hot weather and how crowded Ocean Grove was with all the summer visitors. He didn't mention the extra people who were streaming into town to cover Carly's story.

"Okay, buddy," he said, rising from the chair he had pulled alongside the bed a half hour before. "I'm gonna get going for now. But I'll call the nurses' desk later to see how you're doing." He put his hand on Arthur's shoulder. "You just rest now, Arthur. Don't worry, guy. Everything is going to be all right. Just rest, you hear me?"

Arthur's watery eyes looked directly into Shawn's, and he uttered the only words he'd spoken since he'd been brought to the hospital. "Okay, Shawn. I always do what you tell me to do."

CHAPTER 68

Diane, Matthew, and the crew stood on the sidewalk and asked the lunch customers who came out of Nagle's what they thought about the state of affairs in Ocean Grove. There was no shortage of people willing to talk, and their sentiments were all largely the same.

"I think it's just awful. To think in a pretty little town like this, such a terrible thing could happen. God help that poor girl's parents."

"I'm scared to death. I have children, and I won't let them out of my sight. Plus, how do I explain something like this to them?"

"It's horrible. We're down here on vacation, but we're thinking of going home early. This isn't what we had in mind when we were looking for a peaceful week at the beach."

Within half an hour they had plenty of reaction sound bites for the *Evening Headlines* piece. Yet not one of the people said they had known Carly Neath.

"I think we should go inside and see if anyone who actually worked with Carly will talk with us," Diane suggested. "Why don't I find out if there's anyone in there who will talk, and I'll see if we can get permission to shoot inside as well."

The air-conditioned restaurant was a welcome relief from the heat outside. Diane walked over to the counter and introduced herself to the man operating the cash register.

"We're doing a story on Carly Neath, and we'd like to talk to people who actually knew her. Would it be all right if our camera crew came inside?"

"I'd prefer not," said the man. "People are all stirred up as it is. They don't need to be reminded of this horror while they eat their lunch."

"Of course. I understand," said Diane, disappointed. "But would it be all right with you if I asked some of Carly's coworkers if they'd be willing to be interviewed? They could come outside for a few minutes, and we could do it out there."

"Oh, all right." The man sighed. "It's a free country."

"Let me start with you then, sir. Would you care to talk about Carly?"

"No. I would not," he answered shortly. Diane had long since learned not to take the response personally. If they didn't want to talk, they didn't want to talk. With rare exceptions, there was no use trying to pressure them into it.

She looked down the counter. "How about her?" she asked, indicating the young brunette pouring iced tea into a tall glass. "Did she know Carly?"

"They both work the breakfast and lunch shifts," he answered. "I mean worked."

"Think she'd be willing to talk with me?" Diane asked.

The man shrugged. "Ask her yourself."

The slight young woman came out to the sidewalk, pushing her lusterless brown hair behind her ears.

"Thank you for agreeing to do this," Diane said. "It will only take a few minutes."

"That's okay," the waitress said in a sweet voice. "My shift is really over now. The only thing I have to do is a doctor's appointment, but that isn't until later."

Diane smiled as Sammy signaled that the camera was rolling. "Okay. First of all, will you state your name and spell it for me?"

"Anna Caprie. A-N-N-A C-A-P-R-I-E."

"And where do you live, Anna?" Diane asked.

"Ocean Grove."

"And you work right here at Nagle's, the restaurant that Carly Neath worked at?"

Anna nodded. "Um-hmm. Carly and I worked together sometimes, but not always. Sometimes she would be on and I wasn't. Sometimes I would be scheduled and she wouldn't."

"When was the last time you saw Carly?" Diane asked.

"I saw her Friday morning. That was the last time."

"So that was the day she disappeared."

"Yes, that's right." Anna looked toward the ground.

"Did you talk much to Carly that day?" Diane asked.

"Not that much. The restaurant's pretty busy in the summer. There's not usually time to talk."

"Is there anything you remember about that day, Anna? Anything different or unusual?"

Anna looked up, and Diane couldn't be sure if the pink rising on her face was from the sun or a blush. Either way, it suited the young woman. Diane thought she was too pale. Too pale and too thin.

"Well . . ." Anna hesitated. "Not really. Carly's new boyfriend came in to talk to her, but he'd been by before."

"Shawn Ostrander?" asked Diane.

"Um-hmm. Carly told me she really liked him but . . ." Anna's voice trailed off.

"But what, Anna?" Diane urged gently.

"I don't know if I should be saying this, since Shawn was so nice to me last week when my car wasn't working. He and Carly dropped me off at my doctor's appointment, and they even waited to take me home afterward," said Anna, twisting a strand of her dull hair. "I don't want to say something that could hurt someone as nice as that."

"I understand, Anna. Of course I do. But this is a serious situation, and if you think you know something that might in some way help in finding out what happened to Carly, you have to say it. If not to me, then to the police."

Anna swallowed resolutely. "It's just that Carly didn't like it that Shawn hadn't looked for Leslie Patterson when she was missing. And she told me she was going to tell that to Shawn when she saw him that night."

CHAPTER 69

"Larry, I know it's my first day back and everything, but I'm going to leave early."

The real estate agent looked up from his desk to see Leslie standing in the doorway. It was always painful for him to look at her achingly thin frame. "That's all right, dear." He gently smiled at her. "You must be tired. Good work today."

"You are so good to me, Larry. I didn't do much work at all, and you know it."

"You did plenty. And there will be plenty more waiting for you tomorrow, don't you worry. Now just go home and eat a good dinner and get some rest."

Leslie walked back out to her desk and picked up the canvas tote bag from the floor. She was searching for her car keys when Larry came out with a file in his hand.

"I was just going to leave this on your desk for tomorrow," he explained. His eyes caught the stuffed bear peeking out from the tote. "Leslie, you aren't going home, are you?"

"No," she admitted. "I'm not. I have a therapy appointment. I didn't want to tell you because I know how you feel about therapy."

Larry took off his glasses, rubbed his eyes, and let out a deep sigh. "Oh, Leslie, Leslie, Leslie. I don't know what to say anymore. It's not that I'm against therapy. That's not it at all. But I think you have to make sure you have the right person treating you."

CHAPTER 70

Diane was in the front seat of the satellite truck letting the cold air from the air-conditioning vents blow directly on her face. She was polishing her script when her cell phone rang. Owen Messinger's secretary was calling to say that the therapist could talk to her at five o'clock.

"Gee, that's going to be difficult for me to make," said Diane as she looked at her watch. "Could he fit me in sometime tomorrow?"

"No, his schedule is completely booked for the next few days."

"All right," Diane reluctantly agreed. "We'll be there."

She turned to Matthew, who was screening the video they'd shot in front of Nagle's, taking time code on the sound bites Diane wanted to use for her piece. "We need this interview with Messinger for the *Hourglass* piece, and if we don't get it today we may not get it all. The *Evening Headlines* script is finished. Let's see if we can get an early approval from Range Bullock. I'll track and leave the narration here with you to feed to New York while the crew and I go to Messinger's office. If he sees me right on time, I should be done by five-thirty and back here by about six. If anything breaks, I can update then for the six-thirty broadcast."

Matthew whistled. "Jesus, that's cutting it close, Diane. I hate to take a chance like that."

"Ah, come on, Matthew. You've cut it closer."

"All right," he grudgingly agreed. "We need Messinger's professional perspective, and if this is the only time we can get it, we don't have much choice."

CHAPTER 71

Every one of the young women who sat in a circle in the therapy room held a doll or a stuffed animal in her lap. Unsmiling and very thin, all six of them were cutters.

Dr. Messinger started the session. "Since we last met, some painful things have happened. Leslie was abducted and was missing for three days, and then another young woman was abducted. Her body was found last night."

"I knew her," a childlike voice piped up. "Carly Neath. I worked with her."

Owen glanced quickly from Anna to Leslie, who was already issuing the response he could have predicted.

"Earth to Anna. You may have *known* Carly Neath, but I'm sitting here right in front of you. I think what

I have to work out today is a little more important than what you have to say right now."

Anna shrank back in her chair and stroked her black stuffed rabbit, her face becoming as pink as the toy's nose.

"How do you think Anna is feeling right now after hearing that your experience is more important than hers?" Owen asked.

Chastened, Leslie plucked at her teddy bear's ear. "I guess she doesn't feel too good. I'm sorry, Anna."

"Do you want to talk about what happened to you, Leslie?"

Owen Messinger listened to Leslie's story and endeavored to watch his other patients' reactions to what was, by any estimation, a harrowing ordeal. He made sure that each of the young women felt free to ask Leslie questions and offer her support.

Anna Caprie confessed that, upon hearing about Leslie's disappearance, she'd locked herself in her bedroom. She'd wanted to join in on the town's search but felt too overwhelmed. "I took a straight pin from my mother's sewing kit and cut myself over and over."

This was a good opportunity for the therapist to do some patient education. Some of the girls had been in therapy for years, but none of the more "accepted" therapeutic techniques seemed to be having any salutary effect on them. They were still refusing to eat. And whenever they felt powerless or out of control, they'd find anything sharp enough to do the damage that, somehow, inexplicably, gave them relief. He felt that something more drastic, more dramatic would convince these young women that cutting themselves might bring short-term relief, but in the long run it was an unsuccessful and, ultimately, very dangerous coping mechanism.

As he had every week for the past three months, Owen handed out the razor blades. At the start of the summer, he had instructed the girls to run their fingers along the edges of the blades—without cutting themselves—and to talk openly about how the sharpness made them feel. As the weeks progressed, he tried to get them to "demystify" the razor blades, to divest them of any power to help them.

Now it was time for the biggest lesson of all.

"Anna, why don't you go first?" Owen suggested, gesturing toward the stuffed animal in her lap.

"I couldn't hurt Mr. Velvet. I just couldn't." Anna's eyes teared up.

"Why not, Anna?" Owen asked. "You've cut yourself. Why won't you cut some fabric and stuffing?"

"Because Mr. Velvet means everything to me. I could never hurt him," Anna whined.

"But you can hurt yourself so easily, Anna. Aren't you at least as important as your stuffed rabbit? Aren't you just as lovable?"

The tears were flowing freely down Anna's cheeks now.

"Aren't you?" he pressed.

"Anna doesn't think she is," Leslie called out. "She doesn't think she's important at all."

All eyes but the therapist's turned to look at Leslie. Owen's stare continued to bore into Anna.

"How does what Leslie just said make you feel, Anna?"

Anna didn't utter a word. Instead, she took the razor blade and slit Mr. Velvet's throat.

CHAPTER 72

The girls coming out of the professional building looked shell-shocked and exhausted. If therapy was supposed to make them feel better, shouldn't there have been a more lighthearted energy coming from them? If they had unburdened themselves, why did they look like they carried the weight of the world on their shoulders?

Larry slunk down in his seat so Leslie wouldn't spot him. He'd taken care to park next to another beige sedan at the far corner of the lot, hoping that his vehicle wouldn't stand out to her. He watched as she approached her own car, a dark expression on her face, the stuffed bear dangling by its arm as she held on to its paw.

He saw Leslie drive away but waited to get better looks at the others. The little one, Anna, the waitress from Nagle's, looked especially distraught as she got into the waiting car. Larry assumed that the middle-aged man at the wheel must be her father. The poor guy. He leaned over to give his daughter a kiss on the cheek, and Larry could imagine the words he was saying to her, inquiring how everything had gone, asking her if she felt better. Just as Larry had often asked his darling Jenna.

Larry felt the anger bubbling to the surface as he gripped the steering wheel, his knuckles whitening. He wanted to strangle that damned therapist.

Finally, all of the young women had been picked up or had driven themselves away. Larry went to turn the key in the ignition when he noticed a woman and two men carrying camera equipment walking toward the entrance of the professional building. He leaned forward to get a better look. He thought he recognized the woman. Yes, that was Diane Mayfield. She was in town with the rest of the press corps that had invaded.

On impulse, he opened the car door and got out.

"Hello there," he called.

All three heads turned in his direction.

"Miss Mayfield?"

"Yes?"

"Hello. My name is Larry Belcaro. I have a real estate agency in Ocean Grove."

Diane shook his extended hand. She was used to people coming up to her and introducing themselves. When you were on television, people felt like they knew you. She always made it a point to be pleasant. "Glad to meet you," she said. "But I'm afraid I'm going to have to keep right on going. I have a five o'clock appointment for an interview with a doctor, and he and I are on very tight schedules."

"It wouldn't happen to be Dr. Messinger, would it?" Larry asked.

Diane looked at him curiously. "As a matter of fact, it would."

"Talking to him about what's happening in Ocean Grove, I guess?"

"That's right."

"Well, the real story, the story that should be exposed, is the quackery that man practices. He should be in jail for all the havoc he has wreaked, all the lives he has ruined, including that of my daughter, Jenna."

"Mr. Belcaro, I wish I could really talk with you now, but I can't. Do you have a number where I can reach you and maybe we can talk more about this?"

Feeling he was getting the brush-off, Larry handed Diane his business card, his shoulders slumped. "I've written my private number on the back," he said, with little hope that she would actually call him.

CHAPTER 73

While his sister lay on a beach towel with her eyes closed and his aunt went for a walk down the beach, Anthony saw his opportunity to take off in the other direction. He grabbed his camera and headed north, toward Asbury Park and the old Casino.

Since he'd seen the man slip underneath the building yesterday, Anthony had thought of little else. The guy had disappeared—just like that. Where had he gone? What was in there?

He stopped to take a picture of the big brick structure, careful to center it in the viewfinder. As the Casino loomed closer, Anthony started to think better of his plan to explore inside. What if there was a bad-ass gang or something living in there? What if they were nasty and violent? What if they retaliated against him for trespassing on their territory? What if his mother found out he'd taken such a risk?

Wait a minute! What was he? A wuss?

He reached the base of the building and paused to look around. No one seemed to be paying any attention to him. Anthony counted to three, inhaled deeply, and ducked into the space between the concrete slab and the sand.

At first, the sun's bright rays seeped through, illuminating his path, but as Anthony went farther, the light faded. As his eyes adjusted to the dimness, he cautiously felt his way the last few yards. Then he climbed through an opening.

Once again the sun was his friend as it tried to light the space by way of a hole in the ceiling high above Anthony's head. He looked around, trying to figure out exactly what he was seeing. Moss-covered bleachers and an empty stage, rusted chandeliers and a deserted refreshment stand. He could imagine what the place had once been, filled with happy fans cheering for the acts onstage. It was awesome to think that now the auditorium was filled with their ghosts.

He clicked away, taking pictures of the secret world he had discovered. Then he stopped to look at the tiny screen on the back of the camera to see if the shots were coming out all right. The flash had done its job. The images were clear.

Picking his way over debris and broken glass, Anthony climbed the bleachers to get an aerial shot of the auditorium. From the elevated vantage point, he spotted something he couldn't identify sticking out from the corner of the refreshment stand. Carefully, he hopped back down to investigate.

Anthony peeked behind the stand. What he'd seen from above was the edge of a Styrofoam cooler. Beside it, a dirty yellow blanket was spread over the ground. *Somebody must be staying here,* he thought. Maybe the military guy he had seen yesterday.

On top of the blanket, next to a tattered magazine, lay a maroon-colored ski jacket. *Does it get really cold in here at night?* Anthony wondered, because why else would that jacket be here in the middle of this heat wave? He picked up the garment and stuck his hand in the pockets, finding only a small white card. Anthony's eyes, now accustomed to the dim light, made out "Surfside Realty" in dark lettering before sliding the card back into the pocket.

Anthony snapped pictures of the mini-campsite

from a few angles. And then he got up the gumption to open the cooler. Inside were two cans of diet soda, an orange, and a box of saltine crackers in a plastic ziplock bag. There was also a package of some kind. He reached into the cooler, pulled it out, and tore it open, excited by the sturdy plastic strips that fell to the floor at his feet.

CHAPTER 74

While the microphones were clipped on and the lights set up, Diane chatted off camera with Owen Messinger.

"Thank you for fitting us in, Doctor," she said.

"I'm glad we could work things out." Owen smiled, a bit too toothy for Diane's taste. "The day started with a burglary here, and it's been nonstop since then."

"Oh, I'm sorry," said Diane. "I hope nothing too valuable was taken."

"Actually, I could never put a monetary value on the things that were taken." He nodded in the direction of the bookcase. "All the patient notes that I had been keeping for a clinical study I've been working on."

Diane groaned. "How miserable for you. Will you be able to reconstitute them?"

Owen frowned. "I'm not sure."

Segueing to the interview, Diane explained what

they were going to be talking about. "As I told you in my phone message, Dr. Messinger, *Hourglass* is doing a story on 'girls who cry wolf'—women, that is, who disappear for a few days, only to show up falsely claiming that they'd been kidnapped. I was originally sent down here to cover the Leslie Patterson story, and though the abduction and death of Carly Neath changes the dynamic, we still want the same questions answered for our viewers."

"Okay," the doctor said, smoothing back his hair. "I'll do my best."

Diane glanced at her camera crew. "Ready, guys?"

"Rolling," Sammy confirmed.

Diane cleared her throat. "First of all, Dr. Messinger, research shows that while kidnappings themselves may be on the decline, falsified kidnappings are more common than anyone would suspect. More often than not, these kinds of hoaxes are perpetrated by females. What's going on?"

"You're right, Diane. Despite all the publicity and hysteria, abductions by strangers have actually been falling for years. Statistically, a child has a greater chance of dying of a heart attack than of being kidnapped and killed by a stranger."

"And what about the young women who are faking these things? Why would a woman do that?"

"Many times, it's a call for help. They crave attention. The woman may feel unloved and uncared for. Invisible, as it were." Owen reached for his glass of water and took a swallow before continuing. "Unfortunately, when a person makes a false report, it damages the credibility of real victims, not to mention wasting police funds. It also frightens the public."

Diane knew she already had some solid sound bites. She crossed her legs and continued. "Here in Ocean Grove, Leslie Patterson, the first young woman to disappear, was *suspected* of crying wolf until Carly Neath was abducted. What does it do to a person who is telling the truth when people don't believe her?"

"Well, I can't comment on Leslie's case specifically, but you can imagine how you would feel, can't you, Diane? Feelings of frustration and even anger would be pronounced. And there is also a sense of terrible isolation. You know you are proclaiming the truth, and yet no one believes you. You feel totally alone, and you want vindication."

At his last words, the doctor stared intensely into Diane's eyes, and she felt herself grow uncomfortable. Owen Messinger was a natural for television. His answers were succinct and interesting. Yet there was something she couldn't quite put her finger on that disturbed her. She thought of the middle-aged man who had pleaded for her attention as she and the crew had arrived downstairs. Larry Belcaro didn't think too highly of Dr. Messinger. Suddenly Diane wanted to know why.

"Dr. Messinger, when we were in the parking lot here, we couldn't help but notice the group of young women who had just left this building, Leslie Patterson among them. Were they all your patients?"

"I can't really say."

"Of course not," said Diane. "Well, let me put it another way. Do your patients usually leave weeping?"

"Therapy can be painful, Ms. Mayfield."

CHAPTER 75

"Anything new from the police?" Diane asked when she got back to the satellite truck.

Matthew let out a deep breath, relieved that she was back. He didn't like to admit it, but he worried about her, about everything. That was the producer's job. He'd been taking a chance in agreeing that she could run out and do the interview with that therapist. But he hadn't wanted to seem overly cautious. For the last hour he had been sitting with a knot in his stomach, praying that something else wouldn't break in the Carly Neath case before she got back. He'd done his share of "crash-and-burn" stories, the ones where the details came flying in up to the last minute, the ones where there was precious little time to get all your ducks in a row. He didn't enjoy the adrenaline rush anymore. That was why working on *Hourglass* suited him. He had time to plan and polish his stories, unlike the day-of-air pieces that were done under incredible deadline pressure.

He shook his head. "No, Diane. Now the cops are saying they won't be making any more announcements until tomorrow."

"Well, that makes it easier for us, doesn't it?" she observed. "With no new information, we won't have to update the piece. When are we slated to air?"

"After the first commercial break."

Diane looked at her watch. "Great. We've still got about twenty minutes." She pulled her makeup case out of her bag and began to apply fresh foundation. "Where are we going to do the stand-up for the end of the piece?" she asked.

Fifteen minutes later Diane was standing on the grass in front of the Beersheba Well. The protective gazebo was roped off with yellow police tape. She was not alone. Reporters from other media outlets thought this was the perfect place to do their on-camera closes too. Groups of curious onlookers had gathered.

Across the lawn, the Ocean Grove Camp Meeting Association's Ladies Auxiliary was holding a fish and chips dinner in the auditorium pavilion. Helen Richey smiled and made small talk as she helped serve the homemade fare. But her eyes kept searching the assemblage for Jonathan and the girls.

Since Larry Belcaro had told her that he hadn't had an appointment with Jonathan last Thursday afternoon, Helen was feeling a bit better. Maybe Jonathan hadn't been in a position to have deposited Leslie Patterson at the Beersheba Well after all. But the question still nagged at her. What did the notation on the business card mean?

Jonathan swallowed the last piece of fish and wiped his mouth with a paper napkin. He hated eating this early when he was on vacation. He much preferred to have a couple of drinks or cold beers and then head out for something to eat around eight or nine o'clock. But he'd known enough not to make a fuss with his wife about going to the fish and chips dinner at five-thirty.

After nine years of marriage, and three years of dating before that, Jonathan knew in his gut when something was on Helen's mind. He could tell she was upset that he'd misled the police. Yet what else could he have done? If he had told them he followed Carly that night, they'd surely have tied him to her disappearance. By now they'd be trying to pin her death on him too.

He gathered up their paper plates and napkins and tossed them into the trash receptacle. "Come on, girls," he said. "Mommy still has to work for a while. Let's go take a walk."

"Can we get an ice cream cone, Daddy?" asked Sarah.

"Sure," said Jonathan. "That sounds like a good idea, honey."

Sarah and Hannah skipped in front of their father, certain of the direction they wanted to go. Their favorite spot was Day's Ice Cream Parlor, just off the association grounds on the other side of the Beersheba Well.

"Girls," Jonathan called. "Get back here." There were too many people gathered around the well, and Helen was always reminding him how easy it would be for one of their daughters to get lost in a crowd or stolen by some stranger. He vividly remembered the time he had lost Hannah at the Paramus Park Mall. Those ten minutes searching the aisles at Sears had been some of the scariest of his life.

He held Sarah and Hannah firmly by their hands as they got closer to the well.

"What are they doing, Daddy?" Hannah asked, pointing to the people with the cameras and microphones.

"They're doing news reports, sweetie. For television," Jonathan explained. "Let's stop and watch for a while, want to?"

His daughters were content to watch for a few minutes, but the promise of chocolate or strawberry cones meant more to them than the explanations of anxiety in Ocean Grove coming from the grown-ups with microphones. They pulled their father by the arms, eager to get to the ice cream store. Jonathan had heard all he wanted to hear as well.

CHAPTER 76

After they were good-nighted from the studio in New York, Diane invited everyone out for dinner. But Sammy said he was tired, and Gary said he was going to ride up the Garden State Parkway to see his wife and kids for a few hours before driving back early in the morning.

"Make sure you're back by five," Matthew warned. "If something breaks and *KTA* wants a story in the morning, we'll need you."

"Don't worry, Matthew. I'll be back."

Diane and Matthew left the crew to pack up their gear. "Where do you want to go?" she asked as they turned onto Main Avenue. "We've had Italian two nights in a row, so something other than that."

"How 'bout the obvious?" Matthew said. "Seafood."

"Great," Diane agreed. "I'll go back to the inn to freshen up and get the kids and Emily. You pick a place, call me on my cell, and we'll meet you there."

Fried calamari, broiled scallops, baked stuffed shrimp, and fillet of sole were served up piping hot and devoured hungrily. Diane noticed that Michelle even finished most of what was on her plate.

"I was starving," said Anthony as he popped the last

piece of buttered corn bread into his mouth.

"The sea air increases your appetite," Diane observed. "Or at least that's what they always say."

The adults ordered coffee. Michelle didn't want dessert. Anthony took a picture of the group and then suggested they play miniature golf and stop for ice cream afterward.

"I saw a mini-golf place near my motel," Matthew offered.

All five of them went out to the parking lot. "I want to drive with Matthew," Anthony announced. "I'm sick of being with girls all the time."

When they arrived at the course, Anthony suggested they split the group. "The guys go together and the girls go together," he said. "And the guys should go first. It's sexist that the girls always go in front."

Diane did her best to ignore the tug she felt in her heart. It was apparent that Anthony wanted to be with Matthew. These were important years in a boy's life, and Diane knew her son needed a male presence. She was sure Anthony missed his father desperately. Watching him tee off with Matthew, Diane ached for Philip to be there with them.

After the ninth hole, Matthew and Anthony sat on a bench waiting for the group in front of them to finish.

"So, you having a good time down here?" Matthew asked.

Anthony shrugged. "It's all right, I guess."

"But it's not the Grand Canyon, huh?"

"No way."

Matthew tossed his green golf ball up in the air and caught it again. "I know your mother felt really bad about having to cancel that trip. She couldn't help it, you know. Our boss made her do it."

"I know," Anthony said grudgingly. "It's just . . ."

"It's just what?"

"Nothing." Anthony got up from the bench and positioned his golf ball on the rubber mat.

Later, as they waited at the end of the course while the females finished playing, Anthony wanted to share something other than his feelings with Matthew. He pulled some plastic strips out of his pocket.

"Look what I have."

"Wow." Matthew took one of the strips from Anthony's outstretched palm. "Where did you get these?"

"They're flex cuffs. Plastic handcuffs. I saw the cops use them on television."

"I know what they are, Anthony. I asked where you got 'em."

Anthony paused, uncertain what to answer. Matthew was his mother's friend, and he might tell her. Anthony was sure his mother wouldn't want him prowling around in the dilapidated Casino. But the Casino was the best thing about this trip so far. He didn't want to give it up, and that was what he would have to do if his mother forbade him to go in there again.

"My friend's dad is a cop," Anthony lied. "He gave them to us."

TUESDAY
AUGUST 23

CHAPTER 77

OCEAN GROVE NOW OCEAN GRAVE

Every journalist camped out in front of police head-quarters read the *Asbury Park Press* headline and accompanying story as they waited for the press briefing to begin. It was just after noon, in time for the local news broadcasts, when Chief Jared Albert came out to make his next announcement.

"Neptune police apprehended forty-year-old Arthur Roy Tomkins in connection with the death of Carly Neath. Mr. Tomkins resides at a boardinghouse here in Ocean Grove and is a Gulf War veteran. He is currently in police custody in Monmouth County Jail in Freehold. He will be arraigned tomorrow on charges of unlawful imprisonment, kidnapping, and depraved indifference murder. I'll take a few of your questions now."

When he heard the reference to a boardinghouse, the

ears of the *Asbury Park Press* reporter perked up. "Would that be a boardinghouse for the mentally ill?" he asked.

"Yes. It would," Albert answered.

"So the suspect is mentally ill?"

"Mr. Tomkins has been treated for mental illness, yes."

"What evidence ties Tomkins to Carly Neath's death?" Diane asked.

"Fingerprints."

"Can you expound on that, Chief? Where were the fingerprints found?"

"No. That's all I'm willing to say about that evidence at this point." Chief Albert looked in another direction.

The next reporter spoke up. "Did Tomkins know Carly Neath? What was the connection between them?"

"We don't know. We're investigating that."

Diane called out the next question. "Do you think Tomkins was involved in Leslie Patterson's abduction as well?"

"There would seem to be a link between the two cases, but we can't prove that at this point. I will say this much," Albert declared. "The citizens of Ocean Grove and the vacationers who are visiting with us can feel much safer today."

CHAPTER 78

How had things gone so horribly wrong?

After such care had been taken to make sure there would be no prints, the police said they had finger-prints. Arthur must have been the one who'd taken off Carly's blindfold and gag. How dumb of the poor man to leave his fingerprints behind.

This wasn't the way it was supposed to happen at all.

Arthur Tomkins was innocent, but it was always convenient to pin things on somebody who was men-tally ill.

CHAPTER 79

"I think we need to get another interview with Leslie," Diane said to Matthew after the press conference was over. "Get her reaction to all this."

"I have a feeling she'll agree to talk with you," said Matthew. "This must be quite a vindication for her."

"You know what else we should do?" asked Diane.

"What?"

"Let's Google Arthur Tomkins and see if there's anything on the web about him."

When they typed in "Arthur Tomkins" and "Ocean Grove" on Matthew's laptop, they got over thirty hits, but only one appeared to be what they were looking for. Two years before the *Asbury Park Press* had done a series of stories about former mental patients living in Ocean Grove and Asbury Park. Arthur Tomkins had been interviewed.

Diane read aloud from the laptop screen.

"With no job and nothing else to do each day, thirty-eight-year-old Arthur Tomkins wanders the boardwalk starting early in the mornings. Tomkins, originally from Spring Lake, suffered a nervous breakdown when he came home after the Gulf War, the stress of the war compounded by his fiancée's rejection. He spent three months in the psychiatric ward at the Veterans Administration Hospital in Lyons, New Jersey, went home to his family in Spring Lake, and got a job. But six months later, he was back in the hospital again after he snapped during Mass at St. Catherine's Roman Catholic Church, punching one of the ushers in the face." Diane looked at Matthew. "This is so sad," she said.

Arthur was quoted at the end of the article, and Diane read his words out loud. "After I got out of the VA that time, my parents didn't want me coming back to Spring Lake. I don't really blame 'em, I guess."

Matthew pulled out his cell phone. "Let me check with New York and see what they want."

The executive producer had decided that he didn't want another full package about the Ocean Grove story on the *Evening Headlines* that night. Since there was no new video except the police press conference, the development of Arthur Tomkins's arrest would simply be told by the anchorwoman Eliza Blake.

"That leaves us free to do whatever we want," Matthew said as he snapped the phone closed.

Diane had phoned the Patterson home and left her cell phone number, asking Leslie to return the call. "Who knows if or when Leslie will call back?" she said. "How would you feel about taking a little drive down to Spring Lake? We could get some pictures of the town that police say spawned a killer."

CHAPTER 80

With Sammy pointing his camera out the window, Gary drove the two miles up Ocean Avenue in Spring Lake and the two miles back again. On the way up, Sammy captured shots of the noncommercial boardwalk and the immaculate beach. On the return trip he shot the other side of the road, dotted with rambling Victorian mansions with wraparound porches and sprawling lawns.

"It's absolutely beautiful here," Diane said from the backseat.

The car turned west and cruised up and down the

manicured streets. One home was more gracious and charming than the next. In the center of town, swans swam in a large spring-fed lake, which was lined with graceful weeping willow trees. At the top of the rise, overlooking the lake, was a church that bore a striking resemblance to St. Peter's Basilica in Rome.

"That's St. Catherine's," said Matthew with enthusiasm. "The place where Arthur beamed the usher. Be sure you get a good shot of that, Sammy. After that, let's stop someplace for a drink."

Gary found a space in the middle of the downtown area, parking the car in front of the Who's on Third Deli. The three men went inside to buy some soft drinks while Diane remained in the car and used her cell phone to call information. The operator said there was a listing for a Tomkins in Spring Lake and gave Diane the number. But she wouldn't supply an address.

Diane hung up and then called the *Hourglass* office and asked for Susannah.

"How's it going down there?" Susannah asked.

"Pretty well, pretty well," Diane said. "But I have a favor to ask."

"Go ahead. Shoot," the researcher said.

"Take down this number and look it up in the reverse directory," Diane said. "Then call me back with the address."

CHAPTER 81

At Jersey Shore University Medical Center, the gossip was all about the patient who had been arrested because police thought he was guilty of kidnapping and murder. Dr. Caroline Varga, who was usually so certain and self-assured, was in a quandary. Should she go to the police with what she'd heard Arthur Tomkins say to the young man who came to visit him yesterday? Or had Arthur's words meant nothing really?

"Okay, Shawn. I always do what you tell me to do."

Caroline had heard Arthur say that when she came back into the double room, thinking she might have left her good pen behind. Just as she realized she had stuck the pen in the pocket of her slacks rather than her lab coat and turned to leave again, she heard the words from the other side of the drawn curtain.

"Okay, Shawn. I always do what you tell me to do."

At the time, Caroline had just been glad that Arthur had finally spoken. But now she wondered if his words meant something important. Could the mentally ill man possibly have taken orders from his young friend? Could Shawn be the mastermind behind the abductions of two women and the death of one of them? Was Arthur just an addle-minded pawn who'd carried out the deadly directions he was given?

Stranger things had happened.

Or maybe she was making a mountain out of a mole-hill.

CHAPTER 82

"What do you think?" asked Diane. "Should we call first or just show up?"

Matthew took a long swig of his cherry Dr Pepper. "In this case, I vote for just showing up. With their son accused of murder, I doubt the Tomkinses are going to invite us on over if we call first. If we just go and knock on the door, they'll have no time to think. That could work to our advantage."

"Yeah, I guess that makes sense," said Diane. "But this sort of thing is the least favorite part of my job. It makes me feel like a vulture."

The brick-and-clapboard homes on Washington Avenue were lovely and well-tended. Lush green lawns and mature foundation shrubbery gave the impression that the houses were inland somewhere rather than blocks from the sandy beach. The Tomkinses' house was on the corner, a big gray Victorian with white shutters and a black door. Gray-and-white-striped awnings crowned the windows. Red and white petunias flourished in window boxes and in the planters on the wraparound porch.

"I want this place," said Diane as the car pulled up to the curb. "It's picture perfect. I want to sit in one of those wicker rockers and rock my days away."

"Appearances can be deceiving, can't they?" Matthew observed. "Looking at this place, the last thing in the world you'd expect would be that the boy who grew up here became a man who lost his mind and killed someone."

The crew got out of the car. Sammy stood in the street as he took video of the house. Diane noticed the curtain move at one of the downstairs windows.

"Well, they know we're here," she said. "Wouldn't it be nice if they just came on out and chatted with us?"

"Don't hold your breath," said Matthew.

"Okay, I've got plenty of the house," said Sammy as he slid his camera down from his shoulder. "Now what?"

Matthew considered the question for a moment. "Why don't we get Diane to do a bridge we can use in the piece somewhere? Diane, you can walk down the sidewalk and stop in front of the house and say something general enough that we'll be able to slide it in later."

"I get it." She nodded. "Pin the wireless mike on me, Gary, and give me a couple of minutes to think of what I'm going to say."

She walked halfway down the block, mentally composing her script. She turned to face Matthew and the crew, who were waiting on the sidewalk just past the

Tomkins home. "Ready?" she called.

"Go ahead," yelled Sammy.

Diane started walking slowly toward the camera as she began to speak. "Many consider Spring Lake to be the prettiest town on the Jersey Shore. It is also one of the wealthiest. There is a feeling of well-being on these gracious streets dotted with large, carefully tended homes. Many would dream of raising their children here because it looks like a place where nothing bad ever happens." She slowed down as she reached the Tomkins house. "But for Arthur Tomkins, who grew up in this house in these affluent surroundings, beautiful Spring Lake is a distant memory."

Diane stopped. "What do you think?" she called to Matthew.

He held his thumb upward. "We'll check it, but I think you got it right on the first take."

"Want me to do it?" asked Matthew.

"No," said Diane. "It's better if I do."

She climbed the brick stairs and rang the doorbell. After a minute, she rang it again before hearing someone coming to answer. An elderly man with a shock of white hair and dressed in carefully pressed khaki slacks and pink short-sleeved Oxford shirt opened the door. The expression on his face told Diane she was not welcome.

"Mr. Tomkins?"

"Yes."

"I'm Diane Mayfield with KEY News."

The man stared at her with steely blue eyes but said nothing.

"I'm sorry if I'm disturbing you, Mr. Tomkins. But I was wondering if you'd be willing to talk to us about your son, Arthur."

"Well, young lady, you *are* disturbing me, and I have nothing to say to you. Now, please go."

Diane flinched as the door was slammed in her face.

The crew stowed the gear in the trunk, and the four of them got into the car.

"Well," said Matthew, "it's not the end of the world if we don't have Arthur's parents. It was worth coming down here anyway for the Spring Lake beauty shots."

As the car turned the corner, they saw a woman standing on the curb waving at them. Sammy stopped, and Diane rolled down the rear window. "Can we help you with something?" she asked.

The woman looked over her shoulder at the side of the Tomkins house before leaning closer to the car window. "I'm Barbara Tomkins," she said softly. "Arthur's sister."

Diane started to open the door.

"Don't get out," the woman said urgently. "I don't have much time. I don't want my parents to know that I'm talking to you."

"All right," said Diane, taking her hand off the door handle.

"My parents try to pretend Arthur doesn't exist.

They say if I have anything to do with him, I can forget living with, or even seeing, them anymore."

"I'm sorry," said Diane.

"I am too," said Barbara. "It puts me in the worst place. My parents are old and won't be around for too much longer. Without Arthur, I'm the only one they've got. But I can't totally abandon my brother."

Barbara looked over her shoulder again at the gray house before continuing. "I do sneak up to Ocean Grove to see Arthur once in a while. Not as much as I should, but as much as I dare. I give him money and bring up some clothes, but all he ever wears is that military thing. His life started going downhill when he went to serve in the Gulf War. God knows why he'd want to be reminded of it all the time."

"Ms. Tomkins, what did you think when you heard that your brother was arrested for killing someone?" Diane asked, conscious that there could be little more time for conversation.

"I thought they'd made a mistake. I don't believe Arthur would ever kill anyone. *Ever.* That's part of the reason he had his mental breakdown."

"Arthur killed during the war?" Diane asked.

"Well, he's never admitted it to me, but that's what I suspect. And even if he didn't, he saw others killing and being killed. That's enough to drive anyone crazy."

Diane nodded.

"I better go now," said Barbara, pulling away from the window and taking a small envelope from her pocket. "I have a favor to ask of you. Arthur has someone who has been looking out for him up there. I don't know his address and I haven't been able to reach him on the telephone, but I have a check here for him to help Arthur any way he can. I don't dare go up to Ocean Grove and get involved. You're with the news. Is there any way you can track him down for me and give him this?"

Diane was about to decline, fearing that taking on the responsibility could turn into a real problem, when she saw the name written on the envelope. *It shouldn't be that hard to find Shawn Ostrander,* she thought. And delivering the envelope would provide another opportunity to question the young man.

CHAPTER 83

Two wrongs didn't make a right.

Even though Carly wasn't supposed to die, she had. That was a terrible thing. But if an innocent man paid for Carly's death, that would make things worse.

What to do? What to do?

How to make the police know that Arthur Tomkins was innocent?

CHAPTER 84

Somehow, Anna managed to get through her lunch shift, though she spilled iced coffee on one customer and got the orders wrong for three others. When the replacement waitress came in, Anna went directly to the ladies' room to change her clothes.

She opened the nylon gym bag and took out jeans and a long-sleeved cotton T-shirt. Though Anna was aware that it was too hot for pants and long sleeves, she had packed the clothes intentionally. After the group session at Dr. Messinger's yesterday afternoon, she had gone home and used the scissors on her inner thighs. She had done it again before she left for work this morning and known she'd most likely need to do it again this afternoon. But she couldn't cut her legs again, so she'd packed the long-sleeved shirt.

At the bottom of the bag, she found the Band-Aids and paper clips she had thrown in before she left the house. Anna picked up one of the metal clips and twisted it straight. With one tip, she began scratching on the inside of her forearm.

The cutting helped release the painful emotions, the hard-to-express feelings that were bottled up inside her. But it had to hurt to make it worthwhile. Anna pressed harder against her smooth, white skin.

How could she have done that to Mr. Velvet? No matter how mean Leslie was, Anna shouldn't have taken it out on her beloved rabbit. Anna hated herself for what she had done.

The end of the paper clip gouged deeper into her arm, drawing blood. Anna scraped more and more until she felt calmer, and more in control.

The knock at the door startled her.

"I'll be right out," she called.

As fast as she could, Anna affixed Band-Aids to the cuts, pulled on her jeans and the shirt, and tossed the paper clip into the trash. She was going to have a lot to confess to Dr. Messinger at her individual therapy session tonight.

CHAPTER 85

As they drove back to Ocean Grove, Diane held the envelope Arthur Tomkins's sister had given her and stared at the name written across it. "Shawn Ostrander," she mused aloud. "He went out with Leslie Patterson, dated Carly Neath, and now we find out he has a relationship with Arthur Tomkins. Two victims and the alleged perpetrator."

"A triple common denominator," observed Matthew.

Diane nodded. "Acting as Arthur's sister's courier will give us a good excuse to talk to him again."

Directory assistance had only one Shawn Ostrander

listed. When she called the number there was no answer, but Diane left a message. "This is Diane Mayfield, Shawn. I have something I was asked to give to you. Please call me back and we'll set up a mutually convenient time to meet."

While Diane left her message, Matthew called New York. Plans hadn't changed. They still had no responsibility for a piece on the evening broadcast, but of course, there was always more they could shoot for the *Hourglass* piece.

"It's three o'clock," said Matthew. "How about we break for a while and meet up again later? There's a summer concert at the Great Auditorium at eight. We can get some atmosphere video, maybe get some sound from the attendees about their opinions on Arthur Tomkins's arrest."

Diane was quiet.

"Of course, I could go alone and do it with the crew. You don't have to go, Diane."

"No, that's all right, Matthew. I'm fine with going. I was just wondering if the kids and Emily would enjoy the concert. I'm not spending nearly enough time with them."

Before Matthew could respond, Diane's cell phone rang. It was Leslie Patterson calling to say she would be willing to talk to them again, as soon as possible.

Leslie was waiting on a bench near the beach badges and information center when the KEY News people arrived. Diane had suggested they meet on the boardwalk, knowing the camera crew would want to get some long video shots of correspondent and interview subject chatting as they walked together, material that could be used to run with narration covering it in the edited segment. Leslie and Diane would be miked for their stroll, just in case any question or answer turned out to be useful to the piece.

"How 'bout we walk up the boardwalk, toward Asbury Park, while we talk?" Diane suggested after the microphones were in place. Walking backward, the camera crew recorded as the two women stepped forward and Diane began the conversation.

"You know, Leslie, the thing we didn't get a chance to speak about the last time we talked, on Saturday at the gazebo where you were found, is what you remember about the night you were set free. How did you get to the gazebo?"

Leslie kept walking, staring off at the Casino in the distance. "Well, I remember I had a headache, just as I imagine Carly must have if her killer hit her over the head as he did me. I remember my hands and feet were still tied up, and he lifted me up under my armpits and dragged me from wherever we were."

"Did you fight him?" Diane asked.

Leslie hung her head. "No, I wish I could say I did, but I didn't. I was so afraid he was going to kill me, I didn't struggle."

"So he was just pulling a deadweight?"

"Pretty much," Leslie agreed.

"And then what happened?" Diane stared down at

the planks of the boardwalk as she listened to Leslie's answer.

"Once we got outside of wherever we were, the sound of the ocean was stronger. I remember feeling the air smelled fresher. But it was only for a minute or two, because then he pulled me up and loaded me into the trunk."

"Of his car?"

"I'm assuming that's what it was. I was blindfolded, but I had to curl up to fit in the space and I heard the cover slam above me. God, it was scary." Leslie rubbed her bare arms despite the afternoon heat.

"I can only imagine," said Diane. "What happened next?"

Leslie inhaled deeply and continued. "I could feel I was being moved. I knew we were traveling. I couldn't tell which direction we were going."

"How long were you moving?"

"I'm not really sure. It seemed like a long time, but every minute I was held seemed like a long time. Maybe it wasn't too long at all before the car stopped and I heard the trunk being unlocked."

"And then?"

The women were at the end of the boardwalk now, the old Casino right in front of them. They stopped and leaned over the railing to look out at the water as the camera crew scrambled down to shoot them from the beach.

"And then he pulled me up and out and dragged me across the grass and deposited me next to the gazebo.

I guess that's the same thing that happened to Carly," Leslie mused. "Except she wasn't as lucky as I was. She was already dead when he left her there."

"Let's sit over on that bench for the rest of the interview, shall we?" Diane suggested. The two broke off their conversation as they seated themselves and the camera crew climbed up from the beach and got into position again.

"Leslie, the last time we talked you told me about the dancing your captor forced you to do."

"Yes?" Leslie wrung her hands in her lap.

"Can you tell me more?"

Leslie sighed deeply. "It was horrible. Not knowing who was holding me that way. I used to have such good feelings about dancing. I can remember my father dancing with me when I was a little girl, letting me stand on his shoes as we danced around the living room. I remember how great it felt to dance with Shawn too." The camera recorded as Leslie shivered. "I don't think I'll ever feel comfortable dancing with a man again."

Diane cast around in her mind for her final questions. "It's truly a horrible thing that Carly is dead, Leslie. But it has made the police believe you; it's made everyone realize you weren't making up your story. You have to feel better about that, don't you?"

"Yes," Leslie said in a low voice. "I do feel better now."

"How did it feel to have everyone think you were crying wolf?"

"Awful, just awful." Tears welled in Leslie's eyes. "But I wish no one had to die in order for people to believe me."

CHAPTER 86

His aunt hadn't been bugging him nearly as much this afternoon. Ever since she'd heard that someone had been arrested for kidnapping those women, Aunt Emily seemed a lot more relaxed. She'd actually let Anthony walk up the beach without asking him where he was going. He'd been able to walk over to the Casino again, no problem.

Inside the dank and cavernous space, the mini-camp-site was exactly as he'd found it yesterday. But this time Anthony made himself comfortable on the soiled yellow blanket and helped himself to one of the sodas in the cooler. As he drank, his imagination wandered, trying to picture whose blanket this was and who wore this ski jacket. Maybe this was the place the guy in the army fatigues spent his time when he wanted to get away from things. Maybe he even lived here.

Anthony wanted to know, but he sensed that he wasn't going to find out anything during the daylight hours. He had to come back when it was dark. Then he could see if someone slept here at night.

Anthony slid out from under the concrete slab, his

eyes adjusting to the daylight again. He walked back down the beach, stopping a few times to scrape at the sand with his big toe, trying to find a little crab or something beneath the surface. As he got closer to the familiar beach umbrella, he could see that his mother was sitting there along with Michelle and his aunt Emily. Anthony jogged the rest of the way to their beach blankets.

"Hey, Mom. What are you doing here?" he asked.

"I have a little break, and I thought I'd come down here and spend some time with you guys."

Anthony didn't want to say it, but he was pleased. He glanced up toward the boardwalk. "Where's Matthew?" he asked.

"He went back to his place, but you can see him again tonight if you want."

"Cool. Is he having dinner with us again?"

"No. We're meeting him afterward. There's a summer concert. I thought it might be fun if we all went," said Diane.

Michelle rolled over on her beach towel and held her hand above her eyes, squinting in the still powerful sun.

"Oooo! The Dave Matthews concert at the Arts Center?" she asked with more enthusiasm than Diane had seen from her in quite a while. "I saw a couple of flyers around here for that and I really wanted to go."

"No, honey." Diane braced herself. "I was thinking of the Ocean Grove Summer Band at the Great Auditorium."

Anthony paid no attention to his sister's outraged protests. He was wondering if his plan to sneak back into the Casino would still be doable.

CHAPTER 87

Diane was reminded of *Pollyanna*, the old Disney movie, as she watched the people strolling on the Camp Meeting grounds. Though everyone was dressed in the summertime fashions of the new millennium, there was an atmosphere of yesteryear as they ambled on the paths dotted with Victorian structures. In the summer evening light, everything looked peaceful and secure. Only the yellow police tape that still cordoned off the gazebo betrayed the trauma the town had suffered.

"I'm glad they got the guy," said the first man Diane interviewed. "But I feel sorry that he's mentally ill. That makes it all sadder somehow."

"I haven't been able to let my kids out of my sight. At least we can relax now and enjoy the rest of our vacation," a woman said. "I feel bad saying that, though, because that poor girl's parents must be in so much misery. They'll never have a totally happy vacation again."

After getting a few more opinions, Matthew directed the crew to spray the area for some general shots. "After you get those, you can call it quits for the night.

I'll call you in the morning if it turns out we have something to do for *KEY to America*."

"So, we don't have to shoot inside at the concert?" asked Sammy.

"No, we don't need any more video," Matthew answered. "You can attend, though, if you want."

"No thanks," Sammy and Gary answered almost in unison.

"Why do *we* have to go if they don't?" asked Michelle as she watched the men leave.

"Because, it's something different that we can all do together as a family," Diane answered. "It won't hurt us to give it a try."

The band began playing their repertoire of seaside music. A few measures into "By the sea, by the sea, by the beautiful sea," Michelle hissed to Diane, "Get me out of here."

"Forget about the music if you don't like it," Diane whispered. "Just sit back and look at this place. It's amazing."

Mammoth was the only word to describe it. The most impressive structure in Ocean Grove was almost the size of a football field. Nearly seven thousand people could be seated under the arched wooden tongue-in-groove ceiling. The massive Hope-Jones organ, with its ten thousand pipes, some as small as a human finger, was installed at the back of the sweeping stage. The acoustics were perfect.

As Diane took in the magnificent surroundings, she

noticed one of the ushers at the door nearest their seats. The woman who stood beside him holding on to the arm of his blazer looked familiar. It took Diane a minute to place her. It was Helen Richey. She didn't look happy.

Diane turned back to watch the stage. When she looked toward the door again, the couple was gone.

CHAPTER 88

"It's never enough for you, is it, Helen?" Jonathan hissed, keeping his voice low. He wanted to yell at the top of his lungs. Let everyone hear that he'd had it with the Ocean Grove Camp Meeting Association, couldn't stand living in the tent, and had no desire to be stone cold sober all day, every day. "Here I am ful-filling my obligation to the association, volunteering to serve as an usher at one of their concerts when there are just about a hundred things I'd rather be doing tonight—and you're still not satisfied. I've just about given up on making you happy, Helen."

Helen was glad it was dark enough now that Jonathan couldn't see the tears welling up in her eyes. She followed him as he stalked up Pilgrim Pathway but called out, asking him to stop before they turned onto Bath Avenue. Once they got on their street, the neighbors would be able to hear every word they said.

Jonathan spun around and waited for his wife to

catch up. She reached out to take his arm, but he pulled away.

"All right. I'm going to tell you why I've been harping and nagging."

She couldn't really see his facial expression, but she knew he was looking down at her expectantly.

"It's because I've been under an incredible amount of stress."

"What stress?" asked Jonathan. "You're spending your summer exactly the way you want, aren't you? If anybody's under stress, it's me, Helen."

"I know you don't like it here, Jonathan," she said softly. "And maybe I've been wrong to insist we come here every summer. I'll never forgive myself if I've made you so unhappy that you've done something crazy."

"What are you talking about?"

Helen couldn't stand it anymore. "Were you here in Ocean Grove last Thursday? I looked in your wallet and found the real estate business card with the note on the back that read 'Thursday, four o'clock.' "

"What in God's name were you doing in my wallet, Helen?" There was anger in his voice.

"Jonathan, believe me. I have never, ever gone into your wallet before. It's just that I had stood there and watched you lie to the police about being there when Carly left the other night. And then I compounded it by lying to the news people. It's eating away at me, Jonathan."

"So you went through my wallet?"

"I didn't know what I was looking for," she stammered. "I guess I was just hoping to find something to reassure me that everything's okay." She lowered her eyes. "I'm ashamed of what I did," she admitted, "but that's the truth."

When she looked back up at him, Jonathan's head loomed against the night sky. If she was hoping her apology might induce him to offer an explanation for the card in his wallet, she was in for a disappointment.

"Helen, you don't need to know everything I do. I'm going for a walk," he announced. "I have some things to think about."

As her husband strode down the street, Helen didn't know what she was going to do. But in the short run, she knew she had to get back to the tent and relieve her neighbor Mrs. Wilcox, who was watching her daughters. Jonathan could just walk away. She couldn't.

CHAPTER 89

"All self-injury—be it by cutting, burning, bruising, whatever—is an attempt to relieve pain," Dr. Messinger explained as he sat beside the bookcase in his office.

"That doesn't make any sense," said Anna. "Hurting yourself to stop hurting." She'd gone home to change into a flowing cotton skirt and felt confident that it covered all her self-injuries.

"No, it doesn't, does it? And cutting is a quick fix, Anna. It doesn't solve anything." Dr. Messinger glanced at the clock on the wall. "Let's stop for now, Anna. I'll see you next week."

Anna rose obediently, not sure whether she should be upset or glad. She didn't like the abrupt way Dr. Messinger ended their sessions. Once again, just as she felt she might finally be gaining some under-standing about why she did what she did, Messinger would say they were out of time. Still, Anna was always relieved when the therapy sessions were over.

But she knew that part of her mental health depended on her ability to assert herself. Tuesday night at nine o'clock was too late. She wanted Dr. Messinger to schedule her appointments at a different time, but until now, she had been too timid to say so.

"Dr. Messinger?"

"Yes, Anna?"

"I wanted to ask you if you have another time slot for me. I'd like something earlier."

Messinger concentrated on his progress notes and didn't raise his head. "We can talk about it next week, Anna."

She swallowed his dismissiveness, but before she walked out, she pointed to the bookcase. "Where are all the colored binders?" she asked. "I noticed you were writing in a new one for me today. It's a different shade of green."

"I don't want you to be alarmed, but someone broke

into my office over the weekend, Anna. The binders were taken."

He watched her face. "You mean someone has all the notes you took on me?" she asked, horrified. "Some stranger can know all the private things I told you?"

"Anna, please. Try not to be upset. My notes are in my own particular kind of shorthand. I doubt anyone could decipher them but me."

As she walked out into the parking lot, Anna wondered if she would ever get well. She'd been going for over two years now, and though Dr. Messinger said she was making progress, Anna didn't see any diminishment in the cutting or in her obsession with controlling her food intake. Plus, she was terribly uncomfortable with that razor blade therapy he insisted on using in the group. She had watched Dr. Messinger taking copious notes during the group therapy sessions. That always made her feel like she was being studied, not treated. Now, his notes on her had vanished. Anna felt violated. Was this some sort of sign? Should she start fresh with someone else?

Anna was deep in thought as she threw her bag across the bench seat of her father's old blue Crown Victoria, strapped herself in, and carefully pulled the huge car out of the parking space.

It was essential to give the gas guzzler enough space so that Anna wouldn't suspect she was being followed. The details of tonight's plan were no more definite than they had been for Carly on Friday night. Exactly where and when the opportunity to grab Anna would present itself was unclear. But her ultimate destination tonight was certain.

Remembering that the nearest McDonald's was on Main Street in Asbury Park, Anna steered the car in that direction. At the drive-through, she perused all the selections listed on the colorful menu board. She grimaced with distaste at so many high-calorie choices.

The patron behind her beeped his horn. She was taking too much time. Anxious and tense, Anna pulled her car out of the line without placing her order and found a parking spot.

She tried to compose herself. If she was ever going to get well, she had to try to follow the therapist's instructions. How could she blame Dr. Messinger for her lack of progress unless she had truly given his directions a try? She had to go in there, buy a Big Mac, and try to eat some of it.

With single-minded resolve, Anna got out of the car and walked across the parking lot.

From outside, Anna could be seen through the plate-glass window. Poor thing. In the bright glare of the restaurant lighting, she looked so worried, her mouth turned down in a troubled frown as she stood in line looking up at the menu board.

The parking lot was almost filled, but most of the vehicles were empty. The few customers who had chosen to eat in their cars were focused on unwrapping and consuming their selections. It was simple enough to walk over to the old blue car, open the unlocked door, and climb into the backseat.

CHAPTER 90

"From sea to shining sea." The assemblage sang the last song of the concert together and then began filing out of the hall.

"Good, wasn't it?" Diane asked her group when they got outside.

"Well, it certainly was wholesome," observed Matthew.

"Like something from another era," said Emily as Michelle and Anthony rolled their eyes.

Diane took her cell phone from her purse and checked for messages. "Still nothing from Shawn Ostrander," she said. "I feel like we really should deliver that envelope from Arthur Tomkins's sister to him. Who knows what decisions are being made about legal representation for Arthur? Shawn should know he has resources to defend Arthur."

"You know what I could do?" Matthew said. "I could drive over to the Stone Pony before I go back to the motel and see if Shawn is tending bar tonight. Drop off the money and see what he's got to say about everything that's been happening."

"Yeah, if you don't mind, that would be great," said Diane. "See if you can get him to agree to an interview tomorrow."

Anthony interrupted. "Mom, can I go with Matthew?"

"I don't think that's such a good idea, Anthony."

"Why not? I don't have anything else to do. It's better than going back to that old place we're staying in."

"The Stone Pony is a bar, Anthony. It's not for kids."

"I'll wait in the car. With the doors locked. I promise, Mom. Matthew isn't going to be long, are you, Matthew?"

Diane looked at her producer. "What do you think?" she asked.

"It's fine with me, Diane, if you're okay with it."

"All right, Anthony. But don't give Matthew a hard time. And come in to see me when you get back to the inn."

CHAPTER 91

Anna slid back into the driver's seat. She held her breath as she opened the paper bag and unwrapped the Big Mac. *You can do this,* she thought.

She looked from side to side, checking to see if anyone was watching her from the other parked cars. No one seemed to be paying any attention to her.

She tried not to let the aroma dissuade her from bringing the Big Mac to her lips. She willed herself not to think about her body and what food like this could do to it. She had just summoned the courage to take that dreaded first bite when an arm rose from the backseat and slammed something hard and heavy on the side of her head.

CHAPTER 92

"He didn't come in tonight," the bartender shouted above the music. "He called and asked me to cover for him. Something about helping that mentally ill guy he's always with."

Matthew was tempted to leave the envelope with the substitute bartender but thought better of it. It should be delivered directly to Shawn. Besides, this would give them another reason to connect with Shawn tomorrow, and he might be more inclined to agree to an interview if they had just done him and Arthur Tomkins a favor.

Listening to the band, Matthew wished he could stay awhile and have a beer. But with Anthony waiting outside, that was out of the question. He walked out of the club and went directly to the car. Anthony, true to his word, was inside with the doors locked.

The car pulled to the curb in front of the Dancing

Dunes Inn. With a partially eaten butter pecan ice cream cone in one hand, Anthony opened the passenger door with the other.

"Thanks, Matthew. That was better than hanging out with my mother and my sister and aunt."

"No problemo, Anthony. See you tomorrow. Maybe we can play another round of miniature golf tomorrow night."

"Awesome."

Anthony headed up the wooden stairs that led to the inn's porch, turned, and watched as Matthew's car drove away. When the red taillights rounded the corner, Anthony flicked his cone to the ground, went back down the steps, crossed the road, and sprinted down the boardwalk.

CHAPTER 93

The throbbing in her head was excruciating. Anna tried to open her eyes, but something was pressed tight against them. She tried to straighten her body and lift her head but collapsed back down onto the car seat.

Where was she? What had happened? Her mind tried to focus. The Big Mac. The car in the parking lot. The first bite. Then a shooting pain.

Now she sensed she was in a car, riding somewhere. Over the soft purr of the air conditioner, she could hear other cars whooshing past. She was in her father's car, she realized—she recognized that knock in the engine, and she could still smell the Big Mac.

Anna wanted to scream for help, but there was something cutting at the sides of her mouth, making it impossible for her to call out.

She felt the vehicle come to a stop. She heard the sound of the key being pulled from the ignition. The driver's-side door opened and closed again.

She whimpered behind the gag as she heard the click of the door opening beside her. She felt hands at her armpits pull her up from her slouch and drag her out of the car.

CHAPTER 94

Thinking that he might have come back and forgotten to check in with her, Diane walked across the hall and tapped at Anthony's door. When there was no answer, she knocked a little harder. Still nothing. Then she tried the knob and found that the door was locked.

She went back to her room.

"He's not back yet," she said to Emily.

"They probably went out for pizza or something." Emily panted as she did her sit-ups. "Quit worrying, will you?"

CHAPTER 95

Anthony was getting tired. He also knew he shouldn't wait much longer. His mother would kill him if she knew he had come here. If the owner of the blanket and cooler didn't show soon, Anthony would have to leave. He hoped he could get to his room, undress, and get into bed before his mother was any the wiser. He'd have to try to get away again tomorrow night.

Five more minutes, he thought as he sat on the floor, his knees to his chest, listening to the ocean on the other side of the Casino wall. A rustling sound interrupted the low roar of the water, but he couldn't tell what caused it or where it came from. He was grateful for the moonbeam that shone through the damaged ceiling providing the only light.

He stood up, ready to give up for the night, when he saw the jerky light moving toward him. Anthony strained from his hiding place to see who was holding that flashlight.

WEDNESDAY
AUGUST 24

CHAPTER 96

"It shouldn't be taking this long."

"Relax, Diane. There's nothing to worry about," said Emily as she folded back the coverlet on the twin bed.

"Well, it's after midnight. They should be back by now. Everyone will just have to humor me," Diane said with determination. "I'm calling Matthew's cell."

"Anthony's not going to like you checking up on him," said Emily as she fluffed her pillow. "He'll think you're treating him like a baby. You'll embarrass him."

"That's too bad." Diane found her cell phone in her purse and pushed the number. It rang five times, and then she heard Matthew's voice.

"Hi, this is Matthew Voigt. Please leave a message and I'll call you back."

"Matthew. It's Diane. Just checking to see how it's going with Anthony. You might have gone out to get something to eat. You're probably on your way back right now. But call me back."

Back at the Stone Pony, Matthew sipped a Rolling Rock and tapped his feet to the music. The blaring band drowned out the ringing cell phone.

CHAPTER 97

Hidden behind the bleachers, Anthony watched, fascinated, not certain of what he was seeing. The flashlight had been laid down on the blanket by the bulkier of the two figures. As the yellow light shone close to the floor, Anthony could see the lower parts of the bodies more clearly than the upper. A pair of the skinniest ankles he had ever seen stood on the blanket. Could they belong to a child?

Next to the bare, birdlike calves, another pair of legs were clothed in baggy trousers. Anthony held his breath as the covered legs edged closer to the bare ones. Then he watched both sets of legs begin to sway from side to side in unison. Back and forth, in and out, the bodies moved rhythmically. Mesmerized, Anthony started to rock gently himself and then realized that all three of the bodies in the darkened Casino were moving to the beat of the ocean's ebb and flow.

The ocean. It was just yards away, on the other side of the wall, but it might as well have been on the other side of the world. Anthony's excitement was turning into anxiety. The dancing, if that was what you could call it, was creeping him out. He wanted to get out of the Casino and run as fast as he could back down the boardwalk. The inn he had complained about a couple of hours ago suddenly seemed like the most inviting spot on earth. His own bed, the clean sheets, a hot shower, his mother.

CHAPTER 98

The band finished its set. Matthew pulled his wallet from his pocket, took out a couple of bills, and laid them on the bar. He downed the last swallows of his third beer and made his way out of the Stone Pony.

The night air was balmy, a soothing change from the unforgiving heat of the daytime hours. A half smile on his lips, Matthew felt good. He was satisfied with his day and the work he was doing. But it was too bad that what was such a great story for him was bringing heartbreak to so many others.

He crossed the road and walked south, parallel to the Atlantic Ocean, seeing his car in a parking space near that old Casino building. He stumbled over an empty bottle lying in the street, caught himself from falling, and kept on going. When he reached his car he dropped his keys, picked them up, and fumbled as he unlocked the door. Finally, Matthew opened the door and got inside, barely noticing the dark blue Crown Vic parked just behind him.

CHAPTER 99

In the glow of the flashlight, both dancers slowed and finally stopped their rhythmic movement. One of them knelt down in front of the other, and Anthony watched as ski-jacketed arms reached out to bare, fragile ankles and wound something around them. Flex cuffs, Anthony realized, his heart beating faster.

Now, both hands and feet bound, the tiny figure folded like a rag doll until it lay still on the blanket. In what little light the flashlight provided across the Casino floor, Anthony could see the girl's head for the first time. A little nose peeked out between the blind-fold and the gag.

Anthony tasted the remnants of the butter pecan ice cream cone as the contents of his agitated stomach tried to wretch themselves up. This was no joke.

He had to get out of here. He had to go get help.

CHAPTER 100

Matthew was pulling into the motel parking lot when he heard his cell phone ring.

"Thank God," Diane said. "I've been calling you and calling you. Where are you guys?"

Guys? Matthew thought he must have heard wrong. "I just got back to the motel."

"What about Anthony?"

If Matthew had a buzz on, it immediately disappeared at Diane's question. "He should be there at the inn, with you."

"Well, he's not."

"Diane, I swear. I dropped him off there just after eleven o'clock. Did you check his room?"

"Of course I did," she said shortly. "He's not there."

"I'll be right over," said Matthew as he steered the car back out onto the road.

CHAPTER 101

"Michelle." Diane shook her daughter's shoulder. "Michelle, wake up."

"What?" Michelle's eyelids lifted a crack.

"Do you know where Anthony went?"

"I guess he's in his room." She closed her eyes again.

"Michelle, please. Wake up and listen to me."

Michelle propped herself up on her elbow. "All right, I'm awake," she said, rubbing her eyes.

"Matthew says he dropped Anthony off over an hour ago, but he's not in his room. Do you have any idea where he is?"

"No, I don't. But I wouldn't worry about it, Mom. You know what a little goofball he is."

"Well, he's *my* little goofball, and I *am* worried, Michelle," Diane said. "I don't think you realize how serious this could be."

Diane and Emily were down in the foyer talking to Carlos when Matthew walked through the door, a somber expression on his face.

"Carlos says he never saw Anthony come in," Diane told him.

"Yes, and I've been here most of the evening doing paperwork," the innkeeper explained.

Matthew walked over to stand beside Diane. "I don't want to alarm you unnecessarily," he said, "but I think, given all that's been going on in this town, we should call the police."

"I already have," she said.

CHAPTER 102

The dispatcher had two patrol cars, and they were both assigned. One was at the home of Anna Caprie as statements were being taken from her distraught parents, and the other was on the way to the office of her therapist. If it turned out that the professional building or its parking lot was a crime scene, it was important to secure them right away.

Phone calls to Owen Messinger's home and office went unanswered. According to Bill and Angela Caprie, their daughter had gone to her weekly evening therapy appointment. When Anna left their house at eight o'clock, it was the last they'd seen of her.

Given the fear that this might be a continuation of the nightmare that had been rocking Ocean Grove, Chief Albert was notified at home. He had just arrived at the station when the call came in from Diane Mayfield. Conscious of the media connection, the chief of police decided to talk to her himself.

He kept his voice calm and told her that he would have a squad car over to the Dancing Dunes Inn as soon as possible but refrained from telling her that another Ocean Grove woman had gone missing . . . a woman who could not possibly have been abducted by Arthur Tomkins because he was in custody.

CHAPTER 103

What if nobody believed him? What if by the time he got out of the Casino and ran back to the inn, before he could bring back help, the figure in the hooded ski jacket and gloves was gone, taking the bound and gagged girl along?

To be on the safe side, Anthony decided he should get proof. He calculated the distance from his hiding place to the path that led to his escape. It wasn't far and he was fast. He could take the picture and run, getting away before he'd be caught.

Sliding his camera from his pocket and holding it out in front of his eyes, Anthony framed his subjects in the LCD display as well as he could given the meager light. The image was grainy, but he knew that once the flash went off the two figures would be captured crystal clear.

Anthony wanted to get the face. Realizing that he would have only one chance to get it right, he waited for the ski jacket to turn in his direction.

CHAPTER 104

The patrolmen found the parking lot at Dr. Messinger's office empty. The building itself was locked up tight, and all the windows were darkened.

At the station, Chief Albert listened to his man's report come in over the radio. It was certain that Arthur Tomkins had not abducted this next victim, and Albert wondered now if he had been wrong in his previous suspicions about Shawn Ostrander too. Perhaps he had been so convinced by statistics that ex-husbands and boyfriends were often the perpetrators that he had automatically looked in Shawn's direction. The chief couldn't beat himself up too much for that assumption, though. It made sense, especially since not one but two victims had dated him.

Both Leslie Patterson and Anna Caprie were patients of Owen Messinger's. Could it be the therapist who had abducted both young women? But how did Carly Neath fit that scenario?

Chief Albert didn't have the answers to the questions that raced through his mind. But he needed answers, and he needed them quickly—before another girl died. Psychologically and economically, Ocean Grove couldn't take another death.

They had to get into Messinger's house. If the good doctor wouldn't let them in to look around, a judge was going to have to be roused from sleep for a search warrant.

CHAPTER 105

As Helen watched her sleeping daughters, she felt that her world was coming apart. Jonathan still hadn't come back to the tent. With every minute that passed, Helen was more terrified that her husband had something to do with Leslie Patterson's and Carly's disappearances and Carly's subsequent death. That would make the man she thought she knew so well, the man she had had two children with, the man she had promised to be true to till death they did part—a murderer.

She wasn't sure now if she wanted Jonathan to come back or not. If she confronted him, she didn't know what he was capable of. Could he hurt her—or worse, the girls? Helen couldn't bring herself to call the police either. God forgive her, she still loved Jonathan and didn't want to be the one to bring him down.

Hannah's thumb found its way into her little mouth, and Helen automatically pulled it out again. She tucked Sarah's chubby leg back beneath the cotton sheet. These precious angels were so young, so innocent. How was she going to explain to her daughters what their father had done?

CHAPTER 106

The figure opened the Styrofoam cooler, took out a can, pulled the gag away, and nudged the diet soda to the girl's mouth. Anthony could hear her coughing as she choked on the liquid. Holding the camera steady, he waited for his chance. But the figure didn't look up. Instead, the head was bowed, appearing to study the contents of the cooler.

Anthony held his breath, cursing himself, knowing that he had moved the stuff around inside the cooler. Was the ski jacket noticing that?

The lid of the cooler snapped closed, and the head looked up, peering straight in Anthony's direction.

CHAPTER 107

"Carlos, will you please use your key and open Anthony's room for us?" asked Matthew. "Maybe we'll find something that can help us figure out where he's gone."

"Why didn't I think of that?" asked Diane.

"Because right now, you're a mother, not an investigative journalist, Di. Give yourself a break," said Emily.

Diane, Matthew, Emily, and Carlos crowded into the nautically decorated room, Diane drawing a deep breath at the sight of the untouched bed. The room was quite neat, the result of the cleaning done earlier in the day by the inn's chambermaid. Only Anthony's bathing suit lay on the floor, where he had dropped it when he came in from the beach this afternoon. Diane picked it up. It was still damp.

Matthew went to the pine dresser. A leather case, embossed with Anthony's initials, containing a toothbrush and toothpaste and a small can of deodorant, lay on top. Diane remembered her son's pleasure when he had gotten that Dopp kit as a birthday present two years ago. He had been so proud to have one just like his father's.

Philip. Oh, God, why can't Philip be here now? She needed him. But with determination, Diane pushed the thought of her husband from her mind. There wasn't anything Philip could do from where he was. It was up to her to keep her head about her and find their son.

"May I?" Matthew asked as he took hold of the knobs on the top drawer.

"Go ahead." Diane nodded.

Inside were underwear and a couple of pairs of socks. The next drawer held T-shirts and shorts. The bottom drawer held a Game Boy and a jumble of cartridges. "There doesn't seem to be anything here that will help us," said Matthew as he rifled through.

Diane felt her heart sink.

"Wait a minute." Matthew picked up another cartridge, different from the others. "This one isn't for a Game Boy. This is a compact flash card."

Diane looked at him blankly.

"It's for a digital camera. It stores the pictures. Now all we need is Anthony's camera and we can see what's on it." Matthew looked deeper into the drawer.

"Anthony's camera isn't here," said Diane glumly. "He had it with him tonight at the concert."

"All right," said Matthew. "Don't worry. This card will fit into one of the slots in my computer." He started toward the door. "It's at my motel. I'll go get it."

"Wait a minute," Carlos piped up. "No need for that. My laptop's downstairs. Let's go and stick this baby in. With a few mouse clicks, we'll be viewing every photo Anthony stored on this memory card."

CHAPTER 108

Anthony knew that once the flash went off, he'd have to run like the devil. Willing himself to be calm, he pushed the shutter-release button halfway down to set the focus and exposure. He inhaled as he pressed the button the rest of the way to take the picture. Then, the flash.

In one swift movement, Anthony turned and scrambled away, holding the camera tight, knowing he was being chased. But he knew he had the advantage of surprise and the speed of youth on his side.

He had almost reached the opening that would lead him out to the beach when he tripped over a rusty tin can.

CHAPTER 109

At the Dancing Dunes, the group was gathered around the desk in the reception area. Carlos was sliding the memory card into a slot in his laptop when Kip came bounding through the front door.

"Whoa, the joint was jumping at Club Paradise tonight," he said breathlessly. "Carlos, I should have insisted you come with me to Asbury Park instead of staying in to do that dreary paperwork." Kip stopped short as he took in the worried expressions on all their faces. "What's wrong? What's going on?"

Carlos explained that Anthony was missing.

"Sweet Jesus, no." Kip was immediately sober. "What's going on in this town? I stopped on my way home at the 7-Eleven to pick up a quart of half-and-half for breakfast in the morning and I heard that another girl went missing tonight."

CHAPTER 110

As he fell forward, the camera slipped from Anthony's hand. Frantically, he tried to get up while scanning the darkened area. There it was. The shining metal package that held the proof of what he had just witnessed.

It took only a second to reach down for the camera, but it was all that was needed for the ski-jacketed figure to catch up to him and grab hold of his ankle.

CHAPTER 111

When the police arrived at Owen Messinger's house, there wasn't a single light burning in any of the windows. After repeated ringing and knocking, the front porch light switched on and the therapist answered the door.

"Yes?" he asked, pulling closed the belt on his robe and squinting as his eyes adjusted to the light. "What is it?"

"Dr. Messinger? Dr. Owen Messinger?"

"Yes."

"It's our understanding that a young woman named Anna Caprie is a patient of yours."

"That's right."

"And that she had an appointment with you tonight?"

"Yes," Owen answered. "What's wrong? Has something happened?"

"Ms. Caprie hasn't come home, and her parents are worried. You don't mind if we come in and have a look around, do you, Dr. Messinger?"

"This is ridiculous but, sure, why not? I have nothing to hide."

Owen stood back and let the men enter. They walked through the rooms, upstairs and down, opening closet doors, checking behind the shower curtain and under the beds, until they came back again to the entry hall.

"Satisfied?" the doctor asked with sarcasm in his voice, never expecting they would ask that he escort them outside and open the trunk of his car.

CHAPTER 112

"Who knows you're here?"

Anthony cowered as he heard the desperation in his captor's voice. If he told the truth, that no one knew where he'd gone, he didn't know if it would hurt him or help him. So he said nothing.

"Who have you told about this place?"

Again, Anthony didn't answer.

"All right, kid. Have it your way."

As Anthony watched the sharp, gleaming metal coming toward him, he suddenly found his voice.

CHAPTER 113

With a few clicks, Carlos had the first of the memory card's pictures up on the computer screen. There were shots taken before the family had come to Ocean Grove. Pictures of Anthony's friends, immediately recognizable landmarks in Central Park, a couple of shots of a homeless man who sometimes camped out on Seventy-fourth Street until the police shooed him away. Diane recognized herself in the picture Anthony had taken the night before they left. She winced at the memory of scolding him because she was annoyed that he'd brought the camera to the dinner table.

"Why don't we skip down a bit?" Matthew suggested. "Get to the stuff taken here in Ocean Grove."

Anthony had been busy, snapping pictures at the beach of kids riding boogie boards, flying kites, and building sand castles. There were close-up shots of tiny sand crabs and a gutted fish. Diane smiled in spite of herself as she viewed the shot Anthony had captured of a teenage girl whose bathing-suit top had come undone by a crashing wave.

"Wait a minute," she said as Carlos brought up the next photo. "What's that?"

Filling the computer screen was a picture of a man curled up and lying in the sand.

"Can you zoom in on it so we can see it better?" Matthew asked.

A few more mouse clicks brought the man's profile into clear view. That, and the military fatigue jacket, nailed the identification.

"That's Arthur Tomkins," said Diane. "I recognize him from his picture in the *Asbury Park Press* article. What was Anthony doing? Where was he that he took this picture?"

Emily piped up. "He's been taking walks up the beach. I know he's wanted to get away from us girls, so I'd let him go for a little while. He must have taken this picture on one of those walks."

Next up came more pictures taken on the beach and then a long shot of a dilapidated and decaying brick building.

"That's the Casino," Carlos said before clicking onward.

Pictures of an eerie world popped up on the screen. An empty stage, moss-covered bleachers, and rusted chandeliers. Then a shot of the counter at the deserted refreshment stand.

"Anthony must have gone inside the Casino," observed Kip. "Remember that time we sneaked in there to see what it was like, Carlos?"

"Yeah, that's it, all right." Carlos went to the next picture. The screen was filled with a yellow blanket. A discarded magazine and dark red ski jacket lay on top of the blanket next to a white Styrofoam picnic cooler.

"Next shot," said Matthew.

The cooler was open. A couple of cans of soda, an orange, and a box of saltines. There was also a package.

"Can you zoom in on that, Carlos?"

Matthew let out a low whistle. "So that's where he got them," he said.

"Got what?" Diane asked sharply.

"The other night, when we were playing miniature golf, Anthony showed me a set of flex cuffs. He told me that he had gotten them from a friend whose father was a cop."

Diane shook her head. "He doesn't have any friends whose fathers are cops."

"Okay, so now we know Anthony has been in the Casino. But who left those flex cuffs there?" Matthew mused aloud.

Something wasn't sitting right with Diane. "I can't remember," she said. "Did the police say that Leslie and Carly had been bound with plastic flex cuffs?"

Matthew frowned as he thought back to the press conference. "No. I don't remember hearing that. But that doesn't mean that flex cuffs weren't used. The cops could be holding back on making that detail public."

"Still," said Diane, "I don't like it." She studied the computer screen some more before making another request. "Can you go back to the other picture, the one of the blanket with the ski jacket and magazine?"

Carlos complied.

"Now can you zoom in on the magazine? See if you can get close enough that we can read the address on the label."

CHAPTER 114

"I can't find my keys."

Owen pretended to search, stalling for as long as he could, trying to think of a way he could get out of opening the trunk of his car for the police.

"Well, if you can't find the keys, we have ways of opening it ourselves," said the officer.

Owen let out a deep sigh. There was no avoiding it. He had to open the trunk and hope for the best. With some luck, the cops wouldn't recognize what they were seeing.

"Found 'em," he called, and he led the way out to the driveway. Owen pointed his remote key fob in the direction of the car, heard the familiar beep, and watched the Volvo's trunk lid open automatically. He stood aside while the police beheld the multicolored binders of patient notes that he'd reported stolen.

Why didn't I take care of these when I had the chance? he thought ruefully. *At least I should have destroyed Leslie's.*

CHAPTER 115

As Diane leaned closer to the computer screen, the lettering on the magazine label was surprisingly clear.

> L. Belcaro
> Surfside Realty
> Main Avenue
> Ocean Grove, NJ 07756

That was the real estate agent who had called out to her in Dr. Messinger's parking lot, the one who thought the therapist should be in jail for the lives he had ruined. Though she hadn't had a chance to do it yet, Diane had planned to call Belcaro to follow up with him. But she knew that she still had his card in her bag.

Why was his magazine there? Was this his little campsite?

Matthew was looking at the address as well. "Belcaro. That's the guy I met at Nagle's the other morning. He talked about Carly Neath in the past tense, before her body had even been found."

Diane had made up her mind. "I'm going to the Casino to look for Anthony."

"I'm going with you," said Matthew.

As the pair sprinted out of the inn, Diane called over her shoulder. "Phone the police and tell them to meet us there."

It wasn't far to the Casino, but they decided to drive up Ocean Avenue, Matthew at the wheel. Diane clicked on the overhead light and rifled through her bag, looking for the white business card.

"Great, here it is." She pulled out her cell phone and dialed the number Larry Belcaro had written on the back of the card. No one was answering.

The car reached the end of the boardwalk, and Diane was about to hang up just as she heard the man's sleepy voice.

CHAPTER 116

No one knew where this snoopy kid was, he hadn't told anyone about this place.

But his revelation that he was Diane Mayfield's son was truly frightening. When the newswoman's son was reported missing, everybody would be searching for him.

Worse, Anthony Mayfield hadn't been blindfolded. He would tell what—and whom—he had seen.

He just couldn't be allowed to do that. For now, a gag was stuffed into his mouth.

CHAPTER 117

"Nothing at the Messinger house, Chief," the officer called into his radio once he and his partner had gotten back into the patrol car.

"Ten-four," Chief Albert acknowledged from police headquarters. "What about the garage?" he asked, assuming he would be told there was nothing incriminating there either.

"No, Chief. Nothing in the garage or in the trunk of the car except a stack of colored binders."

"Binders, you say?" Albert asked, recalling, amid the chaos of the week, the day-shift report of the theft at Dr. Messinger's office filed on Monday.

"Yes. Multicolored binders."

"Go back there and seize those binders from that son of a bitch. He staged his own burglary."

CHAPTER 118

"Mr. Belcaro, this is Diane Mayfield. I'm sorry for calling you so late."

"Oh, hello, Ms. Mayfield," he said with enthusiasm. "That's quite all right. I wasn't really sleeping, but I couldn't find my cell phone right away. I'm so glad you're calling me. I was hoping you would ever since our conversation in the parking lot."

"I still would like to talk with you about Dr. Messinger, Mr. Belcaro. But something else has come up that I'm hoping you can help me with."

"Oh." She could hear the disappointment in his tone. "What's that?"

She didn't want to reveal too much. "My son is an amateur photographer, and he's been taking photos of just about everything he's seen in Ocean Grove. He seems to have come across a campsite of some sort, and one of the items in his pictures is a magazine with your name on the mailing label. I'm just wondering, Mr. Belcaro, how your magazine might have gotten there."

"Where is *there,* Ms. Mayfield?"

"We think it's in the old Casino at the end of the boardwalk."

"I'm sorry, I really am, but as you can imagine, I have absolutely no idea how that would have gotten there."

"All right, Mr. Belcaro. Thank you for your time, and again, I'm sorry for disturbing you at home."

But as Diane snapped her cell phone closed, she realized that she had no guarantee Belcaro had been talking to her from his home. He'd said he was on his cell phone. He could have been anywhere.

In front of them, the Casino loomed large and forbidding against the night sky.

"You ready to go inside?" Matthew asked, pulling a flashlight from the glove compartment.

"Yes," said Diane. "Please, God, let him be in there." She opened the car door and stepped out. Together they made their way around the building, looking for a way inside. They paid no attention to the DANGER and NO TRESPASSING signs on the rickety fence blocking the entrance. Once they were inside the cavernous auditorium, the yellow beam of the flashlight shot out over the cement floor pockmarked with puddles of stagnant rainwater. Matthew directed the light up at the billboard that announced they were in what was once the Casino Skating Palace.

"Anthony," Diane called out. "Anthony, are you here?"

On the other side of the wall, Anthony heard his mother calling him. But the gag in his mouth kept him from answering her.

CHAPTER 119

"Anthony," Diane called out yet another time.

"Let's face it, Diane. There's nobody here," said Matthew as his flashlight swept the space. "And maybe we're wrong. Maybe this isn't the place Anthony took those pictures."

"I guess you're right," Diane said as they walked across the debris-strewn floor to the exit. "But where is Anthony? I'm sorry, Matthew, I don't care if there is another young woman missing tonight. The police should be looking for my son. Why haven't they come yet?"

"I don't know, Diane. When we get outside, I'll call them again."

As Matthew pulled out his cell, Diane walked toward the ocean and watched the waves rolling in, her mind wandering to places she did not want it to go. *Anthony wouldn't have gone out to the beach by himself for a swim, would he? There's no chance he could be out there under the water somewhere, is there?*

Stop it, she told herself. *That does no good. Stop thinking like a distraught mother and start thinking of where Anthony could have gone.* But try as she might, her mind wouldn't stop spinning. Diane thought of the parents of the girl who had gone missing tonight and how frantic they must be. She thought of poor Carly's parents and the grief they were enduring. And she thought of Audrey Patterson and how she must have ached for her daughter's safe return.

Diane willed herself not to panic. Things had turned out happily for the Pattersons. Leslie had been returned unharmed. Tomorrow, she told herself, she would be sitting beside Anthony, just the way she had sat and talked to Leslie Patterson the day after she had been released from her three-day ordeal.

That afternoon seemed like such a long time ago. Diane recalled that she had found it remarkable how resilient human beings can be. One day you could be in mortal danger, the next you were planning how to jump-start your career.

Leslie Patterson had said she was going to study for her real estate license. She wanted more out of her job than filing, answering phones, and ordering supplies.

With a start, it came to Diane. The magazine in Anthony's picture had Larry Belcaro's office address on the mailing label, not his home address. Leslie Patterson could have ordered the magazines that came to the Surfside Realty office.

She spun around and took hold of Matthew's arm, interrupting his phone conversation. "Matthew," she said, "get the Pattersons' number and see if Leslie's home."

Diane grabbed his flashlight and ran back inside the Casino, knowing she had to find the place Anthony had captured in his pictures. She had to look harder.

They had already searched the huge, high-ceilinged room, and Diane was satisfied that there was no one there. But from the outside, the Casino appeared a good deal larger than this space. She walked to the wall closest to the ocean, realizing there had to be another part of the building behind it. She trained the flashlight on the wall's surface, looking for a way to get to the other side. Pacing the length of the room, she came upon a loose wooden plank propped against the wall. When she pulled it back, she found the wood was covering a hole. As she stepped forward, her foot bumped into something soft.

Her pulse pounded in her ears as the flashlight lit a worn brown teddy bear dressed in taffeta and pearls— an older, bedraggled version of the bears Diane remembered seeing in Lavender & Lace. Audrey Patterson had said her daughter had had one of the bears for years.

Diane leaned into the dark opening. "Anthony, if you're in there, answer me." And then, she called out even louder, "Leslie, are you in there?"

She heard nothing but the sound of the ocean's rumble.

"Leslie? Leslie, it's Diane Mayfield. Please don't hurt my little boy."

"Don't come any closer" came the muffled response from the other side.

Diane jumped as she felt a hand on her shoulder, but she let out a sigh of relief as she realized it was Matthew.

"Leslie? Leslie Patterson is in there?" he whispered.

Diane nodded, putting a finger to her lips. She then called out again. "Leslie, please," she pleaded, trying to think of how to engage the girl in conversation, hoping if she kept her talking and distracted, she wouldn't be hurting Anthony. "Please, Leslie. Is Anthony in there with you?"

"Don't come any closer." There was desperation in the voice coming from the other side of the wall.

Matthew whispered, "Maybe we should wait for the police to get here."

Diane answered quietly. "Who knows how long that will take? If there's a chance my son could be in there, I'm not waiting around."

CHAPTER 120

Jonathan had walked down the boardwalk and into Bradley Beach, where he'd found a place to buy a beer, and then another, and another.

He couldn't believe that Helen actually thought he'd had anything to do with Carly Neath's disappearance and death. How could his wife believe him to be such a monster?

Yes, he had followed Carly that night. But it was completely innocent. He'd followed her all the way past her house. But spotting that old guy hiding on the porch next to Carly's house had spooked him. By the time she got to the boardwalk and turned toward Asbury Park, Jonathan had made up his mind to go back. He'd headed home by another route, just to avoid the old geezer in the shadows.

True, when the police came to the tent the next morning to ask about Carly, he'd made them believe he'd stayed with Helen when the babysitter left. But if he'd told the truth, that he'd followed Carly, surely the police would have looked at him as a suspect.

Now, as Jonathan continued his walk home, he hiccupped and turned onto Bath Avenue. *Damn it.* He was going to have to tell Helen everything.

CHAPTER 121

"I'm turning off the flashlight," whispered Diane. "We don't want to alert her that we're coming."

They crouched down as they passed through the opening in the wall. Finding their way in the dark was next to impossible. Matthew, who was leading, stumbled over a ragged chunk of concrete and fell.

"I can hear you," called Leslie. "Don't come any farther, or . . . or I'll . . . I'll hurt somebody."

"Leslie, do you have Anthony in there with you? Do you have my son?"

"Stop right where you are." There was desperation in Leslie's voice. "Please stop."

Matthew righted himself, and he and Diane felt their

way forward, soon being led by the glow of Leslie's flashlight. As they peeked around a massive concrete stanchion, the scene brought them up short.

Leslie was kneeling on the floor, sitting back on her haunches. Another figure was sprawled in front of her, hands and feet bound, blindfolded, and with a gag across the mouth. Leslie was cradling the figure's head and shoulder in her left arm, the overall impression that of a depraved version of Michelangelo's *Pietà*. Despite the heat, Leslie was wearing a ski jacket and leather gloves, and her right hand was holding something at her prisoner's neck.

Diane was convinced that her son must be there as well. She turned on the flashlight. "Stealth be damned," she whispered to herself. As the light spread around the space, she was terrified to learn the truth, but she had to know. "Where's my son, Leslie? Have you hurt my little boy?"

Before Leslie had a chance to respond, Diane screamed, "Oh, my God." The beam from her flashlight fell on another figure lying a few yards away, bound and gagged in the same fashion as the first. Diane recognized the sneakers that Anthony had begged her to buy.

"Anthony!" She lunged forward.

"Don't take another step," Leslie snarled, "or I'll hurt Anna. I swear I will. I'll slit her throat just like she slit her precious Mr. Velvet's."

Diane's chest tightened. She ached to run to her son, but she didn't want to provoke Leslie into doing something unspeakable.

"How did you know it was me?" Leslie asked, shifting her focus. "How did you know I was in here?"

Diane tried to keep her voice calm. "Look around for a magazine there, Leslie," she said, pointing to the cooler and blanket. "Do you see it?"

"Yeah. What of it?"

"It has your boss's name on it, but Larry didn't order that magazine. You did, didn't you?"

"You figured it out from that?"

"No, but it made me suspicious," said Diane as she tried imperceptibly to inch forward. "There was something else that had been bothering me. When we talked on the boardwalk, you said Carly was already dead when she was dragged to the gazebo. Only the murderer would know that for sure. If the police knew from Carly's autopsy, they certainly haven't released that information."

Diane waited for a response. Getting none, she continued. "That was a mistake, wasn't it, Leslie? You wanted it to look like Carly was treated the same way you were, and the only difference was that you lived and Carly didn't."

"Even though I hated that Carly had stolen Shawn away from me, she wasn't supposed to die," Leslie whimpered. "No one was supposed to die. I wanted to keep Carly for three days, just like I had been gone for three days, to convince the police to believe me. I wore this ski jacket to bulk me up so Carly wouldn't feel how thin I am. And I wore these gloves so she wouldn't feel my bony fingers. I made up the story that I'd been danced with, so I had to make sure Carly would say the same thing when she was released. But when I came back to the Casino to dance with her again, Carly wouldn't move."

"You didn't plan on anyone stumbling upon your secret hideaway, did you?" Diane asked, trying to keep Leslie talking.

"No. It was bad enough that no one believed me. But things got worse when Arthur Tomkins was arrested." Leslie's voice began to tremble. "That poor man must have found Carly before I came back, and he left his fingerprints behind. I knew he would be convicted because of that. I had been so careful not to leave mine anywhere. I even practiced putting the flex cuffs on myself using my teeth so that there'd be no prints when they found me. The police weren't going to find any other fingerprints, and it looked like Arthur was going to pay for something he didn't do."

"So you abducted another girl to show that Arthur couldn't be the kidnapper?" Diane was getting closer to the blanket.

"Yes, I took Anna. I thought if someone else went missing, it would prove to the police they had the wrong man."

"So you *did* cry wolf, Leslie. Why would you do that?"

Leslie's voice sounded stronger as she answered. "Because I wanted Shawn to realize that he should have taken better care of me. That I'm not trash you can throw away when you're finished with it. I read all those stories, and I saw it all on television. Women who faked their own disappearances. But they made mistakes, did stupid things that convinced everyone they weren't telling the truth."

And you have too, thought Diane, but she didn't say it aloud. There was no point in berating Leslie. It was more important to convince her to let her two hostages go free.

"Leslie, this is Matthew Voigt." Leslie sat up straighter, startled by the new voice. "I'm Diane's producer. Remember we met on the boardwalk?"

No answer.

"We can help you, Leslie. We can help everyone understand that you didn't plan for all of this to happen."

"No. It's all ruined. There's no way out of this." There was that desperation again in the girl's voice.

Diane kept the flashlight trained on Anthony. He was struggling in vain to get his hands free. "Leslie," she said in a soothing voice, "no one is going to think that you meant for this to happen—but only if you let my son and Anna go free. One innocent woman has died. Don't hurt anyone else."

"But how can I go on?" Leslie said hoarsely. "Everyone will know what I've done. My parents. Shawn. They'll all reject me. I've felt rejected for as long as I can remember. Never good enough, or smart enough, or pretty enough."

"Leslie," Diane said in as calm a tone as she could

manage, "everyone will understand. Believe me. Just let them go." She took a step, and then another.

Leslie screamed, "Stop! I told you not to come any closer." She pulled her arm out from under Anna and let her body fall to the floor. Looking directly into Diane's face, Leslie brought the razor blade up to her own throat and sliced her thin neck.

EPILOGUE

As the sun rose over the Atlantic Ocean, Diane stood on the sand with the Casino at her back. Anthony had returned to the inn and was, she hoped, sleeping soundly by now. Emily and Michelle had promised her they wouldn't let him out of their sight if he came out of his room.

She was wired and ready to record her on-camera close. Diane smiled at Sammy and Gary as they made their preparations for the live shot. Sammy was uncharacteristically quiet this morning, as if in respect for what Diane had been through.

Ocean Grove was the lead story on *KEY to America* this morning. With five minutes till air, Matthew arrived back at Diane's side, ready to fill her in on what he had just learned from the police.

"We're golden with the cops." He grinned. "All of a sudden they're telling me everything we want to know. First of all, Leslie is all right. She missed her jugular vein, and she's in stable condition at Jersey Shore University Medical Center."

"Thank God the police finally got there right after she cut herself," Diane said softly. "If they hadn't, who knows what would have happened?"

"Well, surviving physically would seem to be the least of Leslie's problems. That girl is in for a legal nightmare as well as in need of some major-league psychological therapy."

Diane nodded. "I guess she will be tried and psychiatric testimony will be admitted in her defense. But if you ask me, Owen Messinger should get his walking papers. Leslie needs more help than he's been able to give her."

"You said it, and she'll be well rid of him," Matthew agreed, "because here's an interesting little aside. The police told me it looks like Messinger staged a break-in of his own office. He pretended that his patient notes had been taken. Apparently, he didn't like how the results were coming out for a new therapy or something he was working on. He was going to get rid of the files with the negative findings so they couldn't be included in the paper he hoped to publish. That way, only the positive findings would remain."

Diane recalled the therapist telling her about the burglary when she'd interviewed him at his office. That visit made her thoughts turn to Larry Belcaro. The poor man had tried to tell her about his fears regarding Messinger, but in her hurry she had brushed him off, not just then but again on the phone a couple of hours ago. He deserved better treatment.

"And, Diane?" Matthew was continuing. "Anna Caprie's fine and at home, and Arthur Tomkins has already been released. Make sure you include that in your stand-up as well."

Unclipping her microphone, Diane was ready to go back to the Dancing Dunes for a shower and a nap when she felt her cell phone vibrate.

"This call is from a federal prison."

Philip fired the questions nonstop. "Diane, honey, are you all right? How's Anthony? I just saw you on TV. How could they make you get out there and tell the story after all you'd just been through?"

"Sweetheart, there wasn't anyone else they could send in time to do the report, but because I'd just been a part of it, it made the story even better." She answered his other questions, reassuring him that his family was well and intact.

"This call is from a federal prison."

"I should have been there, Diane. I hate that I'm not out there to protect you."

Diane refrained from whispering, *I hate that too.* She answered instead, "We're fine, Philip. We really are."

"If anything ever happened to you or one of the kids, I don't know what I'd do. I've done so much to hurt you already. But if you give me a chance, Diane, I'll make it up to you. I promise I will."

"You'll be out of there soon, Philip. And when you

come home, we'll take it one step at a time. That's all we can do. But I do love you, Philip, and I know you love me. That's a better start than many people have."

"Ready for me to drop you off for a little shut-eye?" asked Matthew. "You can catch a couple of hours' sleep before you have to work on the piece for *Evening Headlines*."

"Yep. Sounds good." Diane smiled.

Matthew gave the crew instructions about where they would meet up later and then the correspondent and the producer walked over the sand, climbed the seawall, and crossed the boardwalk to Matthew's car.

"You think we could make a stop before you drop me off?" Diane asked.

"Sure," said Matthew. "Where to?"

When they arrived at Surfside Realty, the building was still locked up.

"Want to get a cup of coffee to pass the time until it opens?" suggested Matthew.

"Fine. As long as it's decaf. I want to be able to sleep later."

They walked along Main Avenue in the direction of Nagle's. As they approached the scattering of tables in front of the building, Matthew spoke up. "Isn't that Shawn Ostrander? And isn't that Arthur Tomkins with him?"

They went up to the table where the two men sat. Diane spoke first. "I'm so glad the truth came out, Mr.

Tomkins. I'm so glad you've been cleared."

Arthur smiled his gentle smile as he tapped his spoon three times against the side of his coffee cup.

"From what I've heard," said Shawn, "we have you to thank."

"We're just glad that everything turned out all right." Diane turned to Matthew. "Which reminds me. You still have that envelope from Arthur's sister to give to Shawn, right?"

"Oh, God, yes," said Matthew, reaching into his pants pocket. "I've been carrying this around since the Stone Pony last night. I tried to find you there, but the bartender said you didn't come in."

Shawn nodded. "I drove to Spring Lake to talk to Arthur's family." He put his arm around Arthur's shoulder. "We talked about how it's time for the family to come together again and heal. We're going to take a ride down to see them later today or maybe tomorrow, aren't we, Arthur?"

Arthur nodded his head three times. "If you say so, Shawn. I always do what you tell me to do."

Larry Belcaro was unlocking the front door of Surf-side Realty when Diane and Matthew got back to the building. The real estate agent looked surprised to see them.

"I saw your report on the news this morning, Ms. Mayfield. After the night you had, what are you doing here of all places?"

"I wanted to apologize, Mr. Belcaro," said Diane.

"Whatever for?"

"For not taking enough time to talk to you the other night in the parking lot, for calling you so late last night."

"Well, I figured out what that call was about when I saw the news this morning. Poor, poor Leslie." Larry shook his head. "Owen Messinger messed her up so badly, just like he did my Jenna. But that quack will go scot-free. It just tears me apart."

"If it makes you feel any better," said Matthew, "Dr. Messinger has shown himself to be a liar and a fake." He went on to explain about the false burglary and the missing files. "When this gets into the papers, I think it's a pretty safe bet that Owen Messinger's practice will drop off sharply. Even if he doesn't serve a prison sentence or get a monetary fine, his punishment will be loss of credibility in his professional community."

"Well, that's some good news," said Larry, brightening. "I've prayed that Messinger would be stopped. I guess the good Lord has finally answered my prayers." The agent looked at his watch. "I have a guy coming in here in a few minutes, and I have to copy off a listing for him. I've been working with him for weeks—even had to lie to his wife when she found one of my cards with his things. He lives in one of the tents when he comes down, but he wants to find a house in Ocean Grove and surprise her."

Diane climbed the stairs to the porch of the Dancing Dunes Inn, tired but satisfied. She was about to go up to her room when Carlos told her that her daughter was in the dining room.

She entered to find Michelle sitting at one of the tables, a plate of scrambled eggs, sausage, and whole wheat toast before her. Diane sat down and ordered the same thing.

"Are you all right, Mom?"

"Yes, honey, I'm fine. Are you?"

Michelle took a long swallow of orange juice. "Yes. I'm okay. I've been thinking about everything, Mom. Emily and I got up to watch your piece this morning. That Leslie Patterson is one messed-up girl."

"Yes, she is."

"I wonder how she got that way," said Michelle before taking another bite of her toast.

"It's hard to say, honey. I suppose it wasn't any one thing."

Michelle looked with wide eyes at her mother. "I don't want to end up like that, Mom," she whispered.

"You don't have to, Michelle. You don't have to. You, all of us, just have to try to focus on the right things in life. It's fine to care about your appearance, but it's unhealthy to be obsessed with it. There's so much more to life than your jean size, honey."

By the time mother and daughter finished their conversation and got up from the table, there was nothing left on either plate.

ACKNOWLEDGMENTS

From the moment I first saw the tents with their brightly striped awnings reflecting the summer sun, I was utterly enchanted by Ocean Grove. Then, as I learned the unique history of the Jersey Shore town, I was mesmerized. This was a one-of-a-kind location and I wanted to write a story that took place here. I could imagine my characters living . . . and dying . . . in this fanciful and fascinating square-mile village brimming with Victorian charm.

But knowing the setting isn't the same as knowing the story. It wasn't until Jen Enderlin, my editor, suggested the theme of "girls who cry wolf" that things began to come together. Jen is the most committed, upbeat, can-do editor and she is such a pleasure to work with. My thanks to Jen and all those at St. Martin's Press who work so hard: Sally Richardson, Matthew Shear, Ed Gabrielli, John Karle, John Murphy, Kim Cardascia, Jerry Todd, who designed the cover, and Tom Hallman, who illustrated it. And once again I was lucky enough to have the benefit of Susan M. S. Brown's fine copyediting.

Good fortune also came my way in the form of my treasured friend Elisabeth Demarest. When I mentioned to Elisabeth that I was writing a story that takes place in Ocean Grove, she told me she had relatives who summered in one of the tents and immediately offered to bring me down to see them. On a cloudless August morning, Helen and Mil Thatcher opened their canvas home to me and spent their day showing me around and sharing their knowledge gleaned over decades of summers spent in the little town on the Atlantic Ocean. Elisabeth, Helen, and Mil made it possible for me to write this book and they have my sincere gratitude.

When it came time to describe the teenagers and young women in this story, I looked to my own Elizabeth, my daughter, to give me pointers . . . and she did, willingly and inventively.

Katharine Hayden put her thinking cap on and came up with a legal scenario that would land a character in federal prison. Though I know she is impossibly busy, Katharine made time for me, just as she always has.

Again, CBS News friend Rob Shafer shared his technical expertise. You are so generous, Rob.

There would be no maryjaneclark.com without Colleen Kenny. Colleen continues to offer her creativity and devotion, not only to the Web site but to me as well, and I am grateful to her.

Laura Dail, my indefatigable literary agent, tends my writing career with loving care. She cheers me on, gives me feedback and dreams and hopes, and plots with me. Thank you, L.D., for everything.

And speaking of plots, the contribution of independent editor Father Paul Holmes cannot be overestimated. I never cease to wonder at the blessing he is to me. He offered ideas and moral support and enthusiasm every step of the way, just as he has all along. It makes me feel good to know that *Dancing in the Dark* is his favorite so far.

So now it's finished. To my patient family and dearest friends, thank you for bearing with me. Now I can crawl out of the dark, into the light, and dance.

Center Point Publishing

600 Brooks Road ● PO Box 1
Thorndike ME 04986-0001 USA

(207) 568-3717

US & Canada:
1 800 929-9108

RECEIVED OCT 2 9 2007 31 95

DISCARD